Pascal Garnier was born in Paris in 1949. The prize-winning author of more than sixty books, he remains a leading figure in contemporary French literature, in the tradition of Georges Simenon. He died in 2010.

Emily Boyce is an editor and in-house translator at Gallic Books.

D0048203

'Wonderful ... Properly noir'
Ian Rankin

'Garnier plunges you into a bizarre, overheated world, seething death, writing, fictions and philosophy. He's a trippy, sleazy, sly and classy read'
A. L. Kennedy

'Horribly funny ... appalling and bracing in equal measure. Masterful'
John Banville

'Ennui, dislocation, alienation, estrangement – these are the colours on Garnier's palette. His books are out there on their own: short, jagged and exhilarating'
Stanley Donwood

'Garnier's world exists in the cracks and margins of ours; just off-key, often teetering on the surreal, yet all too plausible. His mordant literary edge makes these succinct novels stimulating and rewarding'
Sunday Times

'Deliciously dark ... painfully funny'
New York Times

'A mixture of Albert Camus and J. G. Ballard'
Financial Times

'A brilliant exercise in grim and gripping irony; makes you grin as well as wince'
Sunday Telegraph

Also by Pascal Garnier:

Pascal Garnier: Gallic Noir Volumes 1, 2 and 3
The Panda Theory
How's the Pain?
The A26
Moon in a Dead Eye
The Front Seat Passenger
The Islanders
Boxes
Too Close to the Edge
The Eskimo Solution
Low Heights
C'est la Vie

A Long Way Off

A Long Way Off

Pascal Garnier

Translated by Emily Boyce

Gallic Books

London

A Gallic Book

First published in France as *Le Grand Loin* by Zulma
Copyright © Zulma, 2010

English translation copyright © Gallic Books, 2020

First published in Great Britain in 2020 by
Gallic Books, 59 Ebury Street, London, SW1W 0NZ

A CIP record for this book is available from the British Library

ISBN 9781910477779

Typeset in Fournier MT Pro by Gallic Books

Printed in the UK by CPI
(CR0 4YY)

For Samuel Hall

On est loin des amours de loin
On est loin
'Madame Rêve'
Alain Bashung and Pierre Grillet

'I know Agen, too!'

The guests froze, staring at Marc, forks suspended. He had spoken so loudly he surprised himself, not having been able to get a word in edgeways all evening. Although, apart from his strange revelation about Agen (an overstatement in any case – he had spent barely a few hours there a decade earlier), he had had absolutely nothing to say. Several times, out of politeness, he had tried to make a casual quip, to join a conversation, *any* conversation, but his dining companions seemed to be deaf to his voice. They, in turn, had nothing to share besides profound platitudes, but at least seemed able to understand and respond to one another. As Marc tuned in and out of his fellow guests' exchanges, they began to break down into a senseless hubbub, the mangled fragments of sentences clogging his ears until he could barely make out a single sound. When someone across the table had mentioned the town in the south-west of France, he had grabbed it like a life raft: 'I know Agen, too!'

The hostess coughed into her fist to break the vast silence that had greeted his booming pronouncement and the dinner resumed to the sound of clinking cutlery, slurping and chewing, forced laughter and incoherent rambling. He did not utter another word until he left, thanking his hostess for a wonderful evening as she gave a strained smile and looked away.

The car smelled of a blend of contradictory scents: pine, lavender, bleach and Maroilles cheese. It was the cheese, accidentally left in the boot, that had started it: Chloé had been forced to empty several cans of aerosol of various kinds in a vain attempt to neutralise its heady aroma. Her profile was outlined like a transfer on the dark window.

'What on earth made you shout "I know Agen, too!" like that?'

'I don't know. I was trying to be friendly.'

'Friendly? Nobody cares that you've been to Agen.'

'No. Me neither.'

'You're being very odd at the moment.'

'Oh. How so?'

'Distant, like you're somewhere else. Is there something on your mind?'

'Not really. Did I embarrass you?'

'No. It's just you shouted so loudly, it was as if you were waking up from a nightmare. Everyone wondered what the matter was.'

'Sorry.'

'It's OK. I doubt we'll see them again anyway. They're so bloody boring.'

'You think?'

'Don't you?'

'Maybe. I expect you're right. The langoustines were very good.'

He had spent a good hour leaning on the railing of the motorway bridge and would probably be there still had it not begun to pour with rain. Often when driving he had seen people perched above main roads like melancholy birds of prey. The sight of them engaged in this sad and usually solitary activity had always intrigued and sometimes worried him. You could imagine almost anything about them – perhaps they were about to throw themselves off, or their bicycle, since they usually had one propped beside them. What were they looking at? He had vowed to see for himself and was glad to have finally done it. With the roar of engines and the petrol fumes, it was perhaps not as peaceful as, say, watching leaves and twigs being carried along by a river, but it was undoubtedly more exciting. Your head rapidly emptied of thought and the flow of cars put you in a sort of meditative stupor, gradually making you giddy. It must be even better by night, with the headlights. Chloé was wrong. It wasn't he who was distant but everyone else, all these people speeding towards him out of nowhere only to disappear again in a matter of seconds, swallowed by the shadowy mouth of the bridge.

He was soaked to the skin when he got home. Since he had no reason to go out again, he put on his still-warm pyjamas, dressing gown and slippers. With nothing to do, he decided just to be. He took up his usual spot on the sofa but felt strangely ill at ease. After five minutes, he moved into an identical position in an armchair. That was not right either. He tried a chair, and another, and another, and finally perched on an uncomfortable footstool housing Chloé's sewing kit. He had never sat here before. The living room looked different from this angle. Though he recognised the furniture, ornaments and pictures on the walls, they looked like copies – very good ones, but imitations all the same. The light coming through the window had changed too, turning the sofa a very slightly different shape and colour. It was as if the whole room were in flux.

Mindlessly, he picked up the magnifying glass Chloé used to count embroidery stitches and inspected the palm of his hand. In the absence of a future he saw a fragment of his past, a small V-shaped scar caused by cutting his hand on a broken window at the age of seven. Then he studied the stripes of his pyjamas, stretched taut over his knees, followed by the cracked leather soles of his slippers. To think people went to the trouble of climbing mountains to look down on the world, when a magnifying glass did the same thing.

The house was reasonably tidy, regularly vacuumed and dusted, but it was astonishing what was hidden between the fibres of the rug – tiny crumbs, fine threads, hairs from body and head, particles of more or less identifiable materials which took on extraordinary proportions through the convex lens of the magnifying glass. It would take days on end to cover this pseudo-Persian expanse depicting everything from turbulent rivers to tropical forests and arid deserts. As he crawled over the carpet, he began to feel as if he were returning from a very long journey. It was his childhood he was tracing, hidden in the intricate swirls of the carpet. He saw it surge from the thread like a spring gushing through a clump of watercress. When exactly had he lost it? We wake up one day and all our toys which were so magical and full of life are suddenly nothing but inert, futile, useless objects . . .

'What on earth are you doing crawling about on the floor? Have you lost something?'

'Yes . . . no. I wasn't expecting you till later.'

'I managed to get out early. You're already in your pyjamas?'

'I felt a bit under the weather this morning. I haven't been out.'

'Have you called the doctor?'

'No, I took an aspirin. I feel OK now.'

'You still haven't had the flu jab, have you?'

'I'll go next week, I promise.'

'You really should. Now you're over sixty . . . Especially in this weather. Everyone in the office has got a cold. It's a hotbed for germs. I'm drenched. I think I'll have a nice hot bath.'

'Shall I make some onion soup for dinner?'

'Good idea.'

*

The onions were browning in sizzling butter. He poured in a glass of white wine, added water, salt and pepper, turned down the heat and covered the pan. He was dying to tell Chloé about his revelation on the motorway bridge, and how he had rediscovered his childhood amid the patterns on the carpet. But would she understand? No: she would be concerned. He would have to explain. It would take hours, and even then . . . It was school that had taught him to keep his thoughts to himself. From the first day, he had realised he would have two lives, his outward existence and the inner one he could never share. Chloé appeared with a towel wrapped in a turban around her head.

'Mmm, that smells good!'

She looked so beautiful with the bath steam rising off her skin. Why couldn't he tell her about the bridge and the rug? Tears formed in his eyes.

'What's the matter, darling? Why are you crying?'

'It's the onions.'

'Sure? Not even a glass?'

'No, thank you.'

'Suit yourself. Now, where was I? . . . Oh, yes! So, Elsa fucked off on that fateful September 11 and thanks to those bastard terrorists I couldn't even complain about it. Collateral damage, you might say.'

Marc was no longer listening. He saw the words coming out of those fat, tomato-sauce-covered lips, which reminded him of a pair of mating slugs, but he did not understand them. The hideous mouth chewed up sentences and excreted them like droppings. The brasserie was nauseatingly hot. The smell of sauerkraut, fish and cigar smoke, and the snatches of conversation, laughter and waiters shouting orders into the kitchen made the atmosphere so thick you could almost slice it. Looking out through misted, half-curtained windows, he could see umbrellas passing on the grey-blue street.

'Could you excuse me a minute?'

The stairs leading to the toilets seemed to descend endlessly into the bowels of the restaurant. While he waited his turn, Marc washed his hands. The water was lukewarm and smelled bad. His hair was slicked to his forehead with sweat. The toilet flushed and the door opened.

'Sorry, excuse me.'

'It's fine.'

He couldn't tell if it was a man, woman or bear who had emerged from the cubicle. He went in, pushed the bolt across and sat down. His hands were shaking on his knees. Despite breathing through his mouth, he could not avoid the wafts of detergent, piss and shit seeping under his clothes and through his skin.

Get out, now!

He pulled the chain, raced back upstairs holding his breath, grabbed his anorak from the coat stand and slipped out of the brasserie like a thief. Not until he was two streets away could he breathe normally again. He didn't know exactly what he'd just escaped from.

What would Claude think of him? You couldn't just ditch a friend who had invited you out to lunch. Never mind. He would call him this evening, or tomorrow, or the day after tomorrow. Maybe never.

The roads seemed to be tangled together in a complex mesh, apparently leading nowhere. All that could be said of them was that they had two ends and could be navigated in either direction. Each had a more attractive side where the neon light of the shops spilled onto the wet pavement. He stopped in front of a pet shop selling dogs, cats, rats and birds. Through the window, half a dozen dishevelled-looking kittens were squirming about in straw-lined cages.

Some were scratching their ears, others licking their own arseholes, but none were smiling. He found himself drawn to a particularly fat, fluffy and sluggish cat, whose eyes remained closed and ears flat while the little ones climbed all over him and tussled on his head. Such exemplary indifference would make him the ideal travelling companion for a journey into the abyss.

The shop smelled like a circus, like hot, damp cat litter, a bit like the brasserie. The air was filled with rustling wings, cooing, yowling and yapping.

'Can I help you?'

'I'd like that fat cat in the corner, the one sleeping under all the others.'

'This one?'

'Yes.'

'The thing is . . . he's getting on a bit. He had an accident. I kept him . . . out of kindness.'

'That's the one I want.'

The woman reached into the cage to pull out the animal, who still did not wake up, and placed him in his hands. He was soft and warm, proof that he was not dead.

'All our animals are vaccinated and chipped. Even him.'

The cat deigned to raise an eyelid, casting a slit of green at the hand that stroked him, yawned revealing a largely toothless jaw, and curled up again, as if to say, 'It's all the same to me.'

'I'll take him.'

On the metro, the plaintive meows emerging from the cage

drew tender glances from female passengers. Marc knew he had made the right choice.

'You bought it?'

'Well, yes.'

'Were you looking for one?'

'Not especially. Let's just say we had a meeting of minds. Do you mind?'

'No, it's just . . . a bit surprising. He's very fat. What shall we call him?'

He had not thought about that. People gave animals such stupid names, by and large.

'I don't know. Do we have to name him?'

'Of course! Has he had anything to eat?'

'Not yet.'

'I'll get him something. Come here, little chap.'

'Today, I bought a cat.'

Ten times he had picked up the pen and ten times Boudu had swiped it off the desk again. The pair silently appraised one another like chess players, the cat curled up in a circle of lamplight, Marc haloed with the smoke from his cigar. Boudu (as Chloé had christened him) did not have a particularly playful disposition. He slept, ate and crapped. And sometimes, like now, he climbed up on the desk, nestled under the lamp and stared at Marc with an unfathomably vacant look in his golden eyes. One day, Boudu accidentally knocked the pen off the desk and Marc picked it up. Boudu had just invented the pen game. That flash of inspiration, a fortuitous connection between neurons that usually lay dormant, was still a surprise to Marc. Now the cat never missed an opportunity for a game. Marc was always willing. Despite feeling a twinge in his back each time he bent to pick up the biro, he never complained or gave the slightest hint of annoyance. It was not in his nature.

When his daughter Anne was little and he was feeding her, he had played the same game with a spoon instead of a pen. She too had fixed him with an impenetrable stare, wondering how far she could push him before he gave in; he never did, having no trouble with his back in those days. For years she had tried everything to make him crack, without ever succeeding in shaking the monolithic calm of this father who was as smooth and upright as a wardrobe mirror. She had finally given up at the age of twenty-five. She was now thirty-six. Once a year on her birthday, he went to see her in Wing Four of Perray-Vaucluse Hospital. He did not much like going and she never seemed especially pleased to see him, but neither of them would have missed marking the anniversary of the end of the game. If time allowed, they would go for a walk in the gardens, sit on a bench and stare straight ahead without exchanging a word until one of them got up, signifying there was nothing left to share.

Boudu jumped off the desk with a growl. He had had enough of the game or was hungry or needed a poo. Marc inspected his nails and decided they were too long.

The click of the nail clippers cut through the silence. He swept the clippings into the bin. What if he went to see Anne today? This was not their usual day, and a change in routine might unsettle her. Besides, with this rain, it was not the weather for it. Nevertheless, he put on his coat and armed himself with an umbrella.

'It's not your day, Monsieur Lecas. It's not the 14th.'

'I know, but I'm not sure I'm going to be able to make the usual day.'

'Anne's having occupational therapy. There's nothing wrong, is there?'

'No, not at all.'

'She'll be taken by surprise. You should have phoned.'

'Sorry.'

'Well, since you're here . . . I'll send someone to get her.'

'Thanks.'

A man in pyjamas was sitting with his legs wrapped around his chair, playing with his fingers, mumbling and drooling. Two nurses could be seen sniggering behind the screen at reception. The recently mopped checkerboard floor was drying in patches and the smell of bleach hung in the warm air. Anne appeared at the end of the corridor. She had put on even more weight. She had inherited a solid frame from her mother, but unlike Édith, who was always dieting to improve her figure, Anne had let herself go. She was wearing a shapeless sweater and black trousers that sagged at the knees. Her slippers made no sound on the tiled floor, as if she were gliding on roller skates. Without saying a word, she sat down beside her father, head bowed, her bobbed hair screening her face.

'Hello, Anne.'

'Who died?'

'No one.'

'Are you going to die?'

'It's not on my immediate to-do list. I'm fine.'

'So it's me then?'

'Of course not! Don't be silly. I came today because . . .'

He wasn't sure why. Because of the pen game he had played with Boudu? 'Because I wanted to see you. I bought a cat.'

Anne was looking at the man playing with his fingers.

'How much was it?'

'I can't remember . . . forty or fifty euros?'

'That's a lot. Give me a cigarette.'

Marc did as he was asked. Anne lifted her sweater and tucked the cigarette inside her bra.

'That guy over there kills cats. Birds as well. He says it's his hands that do it, not him.'

'Shall we go outside so you can smoke that cigarette?'

They sat under a sort of canopy. Water droplets clung to the edge of the roof, a kind of pearl curtain hanging between them and the gardens beyond. Anne had only taken a couple of drags on the cigarette she was holding, which had now gone out.

'Have you seen your mother recently?'

'Yes.'

'How is she?'

'She talks too much.'

Édith always had been a blabbermouth. He wondered how time had treated her. Since their divorce twenty years earlier he had only seen her once, when Anne had gone into Perray-Vaucluse. She was as beautiful then, and as much of a pain in the arse, as she had ever been. All he knew was that she was still living alone in the same apartment and worked in the property business. They had never made any effort to get back in touch.

'You didn't bring my Rocher Suchard?'

'I did! Sorry, I forgot. Here.'

The chocolate had melted a little in the warmth of his pocket. Anne got it all over her fingers as she unwrapped it. She shoved the whole thing into her mouth in one go and chewed loudly, breathing through her nose. Marc handed her a tissue.

'Wipe your mouth and fingers.'

All this achieved was to spread the chocolate further over Anne's lips. She had the same look on her face as Boudu after lapping up his milk: satisfied, but disappointed it was over so quickly.

'What time is it?'

'Almost five.'

'I'm going back. My programme's on.'

They parted outside the games room. To avoid getting his cheeks mucky, he kissed his daughter on the forehead. She was the same height as him.

'I don't suppose you'll be back?'

'Of course I will. I'll be here on the 14th, as usual. Today was just . . . a little extra.'

'Oh. What's the name of the cat?'

'Boudu.'

She repeated the word, furrowing her brow, before turning on her heel and disappearing inside the games room. As he left, Marc heard the monotonous pitter-patter of a ping-pong game.

'Twenty euros isn't too much, is it?'

'Not if you like it.'

After Chloé's 'trunk period' – her collection of cabin trunks with curved lids, having outgrown the house, now filled half the attic – she had moved on to a particular style of bedside table: 1920s and '30s nightstands with marble tops, a drawer and a door to conceal a chamber pot. She picked these up at flea markets and restored them lovingly. They already owned eight, spread about the house. This would be number nine.

'I'm sure I can get it for fifteen.'

Marc turned away and lit a cigarette to hide his embarrassment. He could not stand haggling, even when it was Chloé doing it. The piles of assorted objects before him made his head spin, just as it had when he had sat on the footstool and failed to recognise his living room. Things were mutating here too. Watering cans were jumbled together with Voltaire chairs, cattle yokes, china dolls, old wireless sets with lights on and porcelain vases in a scene of such indescribable chaos it was hard to remember what the objects were meant for, now that they had been reduced to abstract forms, morphing together into something truly monstrous.

His hands and feet were cold. This Sunday was already rendering him numb. The insidious stench of chip fat had infiltrated his lungs and the cries of stallholders felt like cuffs to his frozen ears. Browsers rummaged from row to row carrying everything from floor lamps to beaten-up picture frames, tinplate horse heads and bizarre utensils Marc could not even name. All these thingamajigs, whatsits, gizmos had passed through so many hands, been recycled so many times, it was as if they would last for ever. It had been a long time since they had truly belonged to anyone. They were just passing through, take them or leave them. They were sanded down, repainted, given new handles, and off they went again. He had been in a similarly transient state when Chloé had picked him up after his divorce. She had stripped him down, polished him up and found a cosy place for him in her home. After seventeen years of purgatory with Édith, it was a miracle to find himself so refurbished, and he thanked his lucky stars every day. Still, he had resolved to let bygones be bygones and put any resentment of his first wife behind him. His memories of her were mixed, evoking the same combination of dread and fascination as a natural disaster. When Anne was born, Édith handed the baby over to him like a cumbersome gift, something wished for but now surplus to requirements, and ran off with an absolutist Chilean poet. Having never wanted children, Marc cared for the little one out of duty more than love, while Édith flitted moth-like back and forth according to her romantic whims. He approached his fatherly responsibilities in much the same way as his nine-to-five, ploughing on like an ox without complaint. Anne, who was endowed with a temperament as unpredictable as her mother's, had in turn put him through the wringer until both women eventually left home for good, devoting themselves to dubious experiences somewhere else, somewhere he was not. Marc had been thrown by the wayside, rusted, dented, put out for recycling, just like the curious objects that now surrounded him.

'Done! Fifteen euros! It's in great nick. A bit of a polish, a new knob on the door and . . . what's so funny?'

'Nothing. It's a bargain.'

They walked away, she holding him by the arm, he clutching the ninth nightstand to his chest.

The house was still filled with the aroma of Sunday lunch. Wearing dungarees and rubber gloves, Chloé had disappeared into the garage to work on her bedside table. Boudu was snoring in the corner.

Lying on the sofa with his eyes closed, Marc saw himself leaning against the railings of the motorway bridge as the cars roared towards him. His whole body was shaking. It was exhilarating. The sound of the cars whistled in his ears, coming at him in bursts like gunfire or meteor showers. Sometimes, when a passing lorry made the bridge shudder, he felt as if he were lifting off, being propelled into space at such speed that the cars seemed to stand still. Far away . . . was a place he had never been. He wondered what it looked like there. Like nothing, he supposed – why else would it be so far away? Far away, everything is different, incomparable, a new discovery every second. A flaming red Ferrari came flying out of nowhere. The whoosh of air took his breath away. That guy must be going somewhere far, far away . . .

Boudu lay at his feet, a soft ball of dough. He was dreaming. From time to time his lip quivered and he let out sharp little cries. He had such long whiskers, they spurted from his face like a fountain. They would have to get him some more cat biscuits; they had almost run out. He must have put on several pounds since he got here. Before long he would be enormous.

Looking at an atlas, Marc found the very tip of the Tierra del Fuego. Anyone who wanted to go a long way away must eventually end up there. There was nowhere further. This was where land ended, dipping its beak into the water. He imagined sitting on the edge of a cliff overlooking the sea, his bare feet pedalling in thin air. The furthest point on the map must look a bit like parts of Brittany. This struck him as rather disappointing, however pleasant Brittany might be.

Marc closed the heavy book on his lap, puzzled. 'That's a long way away, sure. But how are you supposed to get there? Finding the end of the world on a map is one thing; finding the time to get there's quite another . . .'

*

'It's the 14th tomorrow. Are you going to see Anne?'

'Yes, of course.'

'I've bought her a shawl. Will you remember to give it to her?'

'That's kind of you. It's lovely. I'll tell her it's from you.'

'You know she couldn't care less. Just give it to her, that's all. Listen, I've got a week's holiday to take later this month. What do you say to a mini break, somewhere like Bruges or Florence? It's ages since we went away together.'

'Yes, great idea!'

'Here, have a look. I went round the travel agents this morning. Budapest looks nice too, and it's not far . . .'

'What is it?'

'A shawl.'

'They're for old ladies.'

'Not really. It's pretty, don't you think?'

'It doesn't smell good. It doesn't smell of anything.'

'That's because it's new.'

Anne plied the embroidered fabric between her fat red fingers. She had the hands of a labourer: big, strong and without fingernails to speak of. Hands like tools.

'What are we doing?'

'A walk round the gardens? A Rocher Suchard? A cigarette?'

'OK. I'll put my boots on; the ground's wet.'

Trees stretched before them, creaking into the void. Engine noise from some distant piece of farm machinery carved the silence into regular chunks. From time to time, Anne strayed off the gravel path to trudge across the boggy grass.

'Welly boots are good. You can go anywhere in them.'

'Where's anywhere, for you?'

'Right here.'

She put her feet together and jumped into a muddy puddle.

'Careful, Anne! I'm right next to you . . . Listen, how about going for a drive?'

'With you? Outside?'

'Yes, with me, outside.'

'I'm not allowed.'

'You are if you're with me.'

She looked up at him suspiciously, arms buried elbow-deep in the pockets of her parka, hopping from side to side like a dancing bear.

'I don't know.'

'You needn't worry, I'll be there with you. We could go and see the sea?'

'The sea?'

'Yes. We could walk on the sand, look at things moving about in rockpools, just like when you were little.'

Anne shrugged several times and sniffed, her eyes darting from left to right and up and down like a cornered animal.

'Which sea?'

'Whichever's nearest. How about Le Touquet?'

'Le Touquet . . .'

Doctor Soyons, who was falling asleep at his desk in a wine-scented fug, did not take much persuading. As a formality, he informed Marc of the risks he was taking and asked him to sign a discharge note. Then he saw him off with a limp wave of the hand.

*

'Put your seatbelt on. There. OK?'

'Yes. It's tight. Who's that in the back?'

'Boudu. He's coming with us.'

'Oh.'

Through the bars of his cage on the back seat, the cat wrinkled his nose and fixed Anne with a stare as glassy as her own.

They arrived about seven in the evening and Marc had no trouble finding a hotel by the beach. At this time of year, Le Touquet was a ghost town. Closed shutters lined the seafront. Knowing his daughter's behaviour could be unpredictable, he had thought it wise to have dinner delivered to their room rather than eat in the restaurant. Anne did not seem best pleased.

'Why not in the restaurant?'

'Aren't you tired?'

'No.'

'OK, fine. Mademoiselle, we've changed our minds, we'll be eating in the restaurant.'

The bedroom was spacious with French windows overlooking the sea, of which the only part visible at this hour was a slim roll of foam dissecting the darkness. Anne pressed her forehead against the black glass.

'We're not by the sea. It's miles away.'

'It must be low tide. It'll come back in.'

'What would you know?'

'It goes out and comes in again. That's how it is.'

'That's how it is . . . That's how it is . . . It might not always be.'

'We can go for a walk along the beach tomorrow. You'll see it then. Ready?'

The few other diners in the restaurant were couples, retirees or businessmen with their secretaries, all speaking in hushed tones. Contrary to Marc's fears, Anne's table manners were exemplary: she held her knife and fork correctly and refrained from stuffing herself or making inappropriate noises. Occasionally she threw furtive glances in the direction of the other tables or stared intently at the chandeliers, their sparkle reflected in her eyes. Looking at her, Marc was reminded of long-ago Christmases when Anne was five or six, wide-eyed, soaking it all in.

'Everything all right?'

Anne turned towards the mirror to her left, shrugged, and plunged her spoon back into the *île flottante* she had just started eating.

'I'm ugly.'

It was just an observation. Nothing in her face suggested the slightest emotion. She said, 'I'm ugly', as one might say 'That's a pebble', or a bike or tyre.

'If you like, we could buy you some clothes tomorrow and go to the hairdresser.'

'If you like.'

When they left the table, the bowl which had held the *île flottante* was as clean as if it had just come out of the dishwasher. Anne let out a loud, clear burp. This was her one misstep. When they reached the bedroom, she took a napkin from her pocket containing some leftover fish and offered it to Boudu. The cat's eyes misted with eternal gratitude, and he spent the night curled up against her.

Despite the stick-thin shop assistants laughing behind her back, Anne would not be swayed in her dubious choice of clothing.

'The red trousers. The yellow jumper. The green coat. The shiny boots.'

She didn't hesitate for a second before the rails: 'That, that and that.' Her pointing index finger brooked no argument.

It went much the same at the hairdresser.

'Frizzy.'

'You mean you'd like it curled?'

'No, frizzy. Like an Afro.'

'Oh . . . but you have lovely natural hair.'

'Frizzy and yellow.'

Marc felt as if he were watching an island emerge.

There was no one on the beach, but thousands of footsteps had pummelled the sand. Anne pointed them out.

'Where are they all?'

'I don't know. They've gone.'

'They were in a hurry. Always rushing to keep going. Because if they stop, they'll die.'

Anne turned around and began walking backwards, keeping her eyes on her father.

'It's weird – I've always felt like I'm on my own whenever I'm with you.'

'I'm sorry.'

'Why? It's good to be on your own with someone. You don't feel you have to talk. You should walk like this.'

'Backwards?'

'Yeah. I saw it in a western. It tricks the people running after you.'

'No one's running after us . . .'

'You can't see them; they're hiding. But I can see them.'

The wind flattened her hood against her head, the fur trim framing her face like a chestnut burr.

'You came to pick me up from Gare Saint-Lazare once. I'd been to Trouville with Aunt Judith. We almost lost each other at the station. You had the same look on your face as you do now.'

'What look is that?'

'A look of "What the hell am I doing here?"'

For the first time in years he watched his daughter burst out laughing as she walked away, motioning towards the line of foam separating the grey sea and sky. Except for Anne, dressed in her new polychrome outfit, everything around them was a shade of grey as subtly differentiated as the waves of mother-of-pearl inside an oyster shell. Marc had always been fond of grey: it was the perfect compromise between black and white and its variations were endless. Why was there no grey-like word between yes and no? Something like 'maybe', only subtler.

It was strange how the rows of closed shutters along the beachfront resembled a craggy cliff face that mirrored the pattern of footprints in the sand. There had been life here once, but it was hard to say when exactly . . . He had not phoned Chloé the night before. When he set off, he had left a note on the coffee table telling her he was going away for a couple of days with Anne, without mentioning where they were going (he didn't know himself before opting for Le Touquet at random). He had signed off with a promise to ring her as soon as they arrived. He had thought about it but had not done it. She would certainly be worrying, but he could not call her – to do so would almost be in bad taste. Chloé was not in the script; there was no part for her, not even on the telephone. Excluding her was not a conscious decision; it was just the way it was, like the invisible presences on the beach and the empty apartments. It was true it felt good to be on your own with someone.

Anne ran back over to him. Her eyes, nose and lips were shining, polished by the sea air.

'You look like an Eskimo.'

'I'm hungry, I need to pee and I'm tired.'

Boudu had found himself a worthy napping partner in Anne. Feeling slightly left out at the sight of them snuggled up, competing for who could snore the loudest, Marc set out on a walk round town by himself. Besides the vandalised window of a Catholic charity centre (boarded up and showing traces of a fire), notable sights were few and far between. All roads led stubbornly back to the beach: Le Touquet had nothing else to offer. A pool of sunlight was emanating from somewhere, but didn't provide any warmth or cast a shadow. Looking for some human contact, Marc entered a Monoprix. Octogenarian couples in ill-fitting Lacoste tracksuits haunted the aisles, over-sized trolleys rattling with yogurts, chocolate, biscuits and other sweet treats they bought to pass the time. Marc picked up tins of food for Boudu – rabbit, liver mousse, salmon – and for Anne, Rocher Suchard chocolates. Then he retreated to a bar – overlooking the sea, obviously – and ordered a hot toddy, swiftly followed by another. He felt the need to fill a void that had opened inside him unnoticed, a void into which he seemed to have fallen when he set off with Anne.

At first he had found the idea of running away amusing – but it was only an idea. Now they were here, it was another story. For years he had been content with plans that came to nothing: learning Italian, visiting the islands of Saint Pierre and Miquelon, wearing a wide-brimmed hat . . . All great ideas, but as for putting them into practice . . . The strange helplessness he now felt was largely because of Anne. The total self-assurance she had displayed in the clothes shops, at the hairdresser and the restaurant had confused him. But what, after all, had he been expecting? That she would go around dribbling everywhere and sticking her fingers up her nose? Roll her eyes, pull out handfuls of hair and let out high-pitched screams? Of course not. But, given her condition, he had expected she might seem a little fragile or withdrawn – after all, her only contact with the world these days came from watching TV and rare visits from her father or mother. Oddly enough, it was he who was feeling vulnerable. This morning on the beach, she had been like a caryatid keeping her head up under the weight of the sky, while he was buffeted by the wind like an old man trying to beat his way through a crowd. He ordered a third hot toddy to rouse himself from his chair.

It was already dark outside. Thanks to the hot toddies, no doubt, every streetlamp, neon sign, headlight and star twinkled like magical candy canes on a Christmas tree.

Back at the hotel he found Anne sitting on a barstool, talking to the barman.

'Papa, let me introduce you. Désiré, this is my father, Marc.'

'Good evening, Monsieur.'

'Pleased to meet you.'

'Désiré is from Togo. It's in Africa.'

The palm of his hand was pink and soft, his smile, eyes and shirt an incandescent white. There was very little black about him.

'A glass of champagne, like your daughter?'

'No, thank you. It's drizzling outside and I'm chilled to the bone. I'm going to head up and change for dinner.'

'I'll come with you. See you later, Désiré.'

'See you later, Mademoiselle.'

In the lift, Anne smiled at herself in the mirror.

'See, I made a friend.'

'He seems very nice.'

'Yes. You smell like a sailor – salt and rum.'

'I had a hot toddy. I think I've caught a cold. As for you, should you be drinking champagne, with your medication . . .?'

'You're right. I'll stop the medication.'

'I bought you a Rocher Suchard.'

'I'm giving those up too. I want to be thin.'

The room smelled of cigarettes. Anne shut herself in the bathroom and Marc threw open the window. A cloud of fog swirled into the room. A light, perhaps from a ship, was flickering in the darkness. Or was it a star? Marc took a tin of cat food out of the plastic bag and opened it, calling Boudu. The cat ought to have appeared at the sound of the lid lifting, ears pricked up, whiskers poised, lips quivering.

Nothing. Marc banged the tin.

'Boudu? . . . Boudu?'

He looked under the beds and pillows, inside the wardrobe, on the balcony – not a whisper of a cat.

Marc knocked on the bathroom door.

'Anne?'

'Yes?'

'Boudu's not in there with you, is he?'

'No.'

'He's not in the room.'

'Oh.'

'You didn't leave the door open, did you?'

'No. Oh, yes! Before I came downstairs. I'd forgotten my cigarettes.'

'He must have snuck out.'

'Yes. He can't have gone far.'

'No. I'll call down to reception, ask them to keep an eye out.'

It wasn't the end of the world – the cat would be prowling round the hotel somewhere – but Marc was nonetheless annoyed. There was a strong fishy smell coming from the open tin. He closed it and slipped it back inside the Monoprix bag.

Anne was wearing a dress bought that morning, in a fuchsia pink so vivid it remained imprinted on the retina long after you had stopped looking at it.

'What do you think?'

'Dazzling.'

As they emerged from the lift, a couple hesitated to step inside, choked by the perfume in which Anne had doused herself.

'Go and sit down, Anne. I'll just let reception know about Boudu and I'll come and find you.'

As he headed towards the entrance hall, Marc found himself irresistibly drawn towards the door. It was as if an invisible hand were pushing him while a voice whispered 'Get out! Run while you can! Leave, get in your car and keep driving, don't stop.'

Of course, he did not act upon this. There wasn't any sense in it. And yet, as he told the receptionist about the missing cat, he was sure he had just missed the opportunity of a lifetime.

Anne was munching through the crudités, Marc was

carefully dissecting his sole and the bottle of white wine was half empty.

'What do you think of Désiré?'

'I told you, he seems nice.'

'To look at, I mean.'

'He's a good-looking young man.'

'I want to have sex with him.'

'Slow down a bit. Don't you think you'd better ask him first?'

'Why would he turn me down? I'm pretty now, aren't I?'

'Very, but . . . It doesn't work like that. You need to give it time.'

'Do you know how long it's been since I had sex?'

Marc did not reply.

'You don't care.'

'No, I understand, it's just . . .'

'What about you? When did you last get laid?'

'I don't know.'

'Two days? Two months? Two years?'

'I don't know, Anne! Can we talk about something else?'

'It's been three years for me. It was with a nurse. He was fired. Karl, his name was Karl, or Charles . . . I can't remember. He had a face like the back end of a bus, but a lovely, bright-red cock.'

'Please, Anne.'

'Yes, he was ugly, but I wanted him so badly . . . Have you ever done it with someone hideous?'

'Probably. I can't remember.'

'I can. Even in the dark, ugly people are still ugly. But it doesn't matter, when you're in the mood . . . Hey, the lady wants to talk to you.'

The receptionist was hanging back at a respectful distance, three steps away, trying to avoid interrupting their conversation.

'We've found your cat.'

Marc stood up and followed the young woman, whose slight limp stirred him unexpectedly. She led him into the laundry room, where he found Boudu nestling against the attendant's ample bosom.

'He was tangled up inside a pillowcase.'

'A pillowcase?'

'Yes. I don't know how he got in there. Looked as if he might've been shoved inside. He didn't seem scared, he was just meowing quietly. He's a cuddly little thing.'

'Yes, very. Thank you very much, Madame. We must have left our door open and he seized his chance.'

Boudu passed from the laundress's arms to Marc's, purring all the while, eyes half closed.

'I'll take him upstairs. We'll be more careful in future. Thanks again.'

Back in the room, Marc put Boudu down on Anne's bed, but against all expectations, instead of continuing the slumber even his trip to the laundry room had not interrupted, the cat stretched out with a growl and went to sit on Marc's bed instead. This unusual initiative, for an animal who normally displayed none, aroused a vague sense of suspicion in his master. Marc checked to see if there were any pillowcases missing. They were all present and correct. Relieved, he left the opened tin of salmon cat food near the cat and left the room.

The bed sighed as Anne threw herself on it with arms outspread. Marc staggered into the bathroom.

'Oh look! The little fucker's back!'

Sensing himself being talked about, Boudu raised an eyelid and pricked up his ears.

'Where did you find him?'

'In the laundry room.'

'They found one in the laundry room of the hospital once, too. But after it had gone through the washing machine. It was at least twenty centimetres bigger.'

The cat arched his back as Anne persisted in stroking him, before jumping off Marc's bed to rub against her.

'He really is thick, this cat. Marc?'

'Yes.'

'Are you pissed?'

'A bit.'

'Me too. I like it. Did you ring Chloé?'

'Yes, of course. She sends her love.'

'Liar.'

Marc got up in the night. He was cold. Anne and Boudu

had synchronised their snoring so effectively he felt as if he were lying in a ship's cabin next to the engine room. As he searched the wardrobe for a blanket, he saw that of the two spare pillows, one was missing a case.

Kites twirled like commas in a sky so clear you could see into its depths. Some flew so high it looked as if they would never come down, but in the end their strings always pulled them back to the beach where they jolted, clumsy and pitiful when not in the air. Fat little people bundled up in garish coats pulled the kites towards them, laughing. Marc felt like giving them a slap. In their chubby hands, the kites were no more than skinny, floundering flat fish. As the tiny, arrogant cosmonauts trampled the grey sand, their fathers ran towards them, big and stupid, drunk on themselves and their progeny, kneeling before the remains of the great birds now reduced to silk squares on a pair of sticks. If only someone would invent special scissors to cut the strings that bind us so tightly to one another – and abolish the laws of gravity while they're at it.

Marc was convinced that Anne had tried to get rid of Boudu: the missing pillowcase was proof. Yet he had left them curled up together when he left the room an hour earlier. We all become attached. The victim to his tormentor, the tormentor to his victim, the father to his child, the child to his kite . . . All attached. All strung together . . . After discovering the absent pillowcase, Marc looked out at the cloudless sky to see a web of threads stretched between the stars, the way the signs of the zodiac are depicted in astrology books. Only here, all the figurative symbols had disappeared, replaced by tangled lines like a doodle you might draw while on the phone, a meaningless scribble in which only the Great Bear remained, recognisable by its saucepan shape. Chloé had once bought a picture like this at a flea market, a hideous object with gold thread embroidered on a black velvet background in the shape of a horse's head.

'What do you think?'

'It's . . . very kitsch.'

'I love it!'

She had hung it in the loo, behind the door, facing the toilet. It was fine if he was taking a piss, otherwise . . . A horse's head?

Chloé . . . He typed her number into his mobile and let it ring a dozen times before hanging up. Of course she could no longer answer him, because she was no longer part of the story. He should have made a run for it yesterday, should have answered the call of the revolving doors as he approached reception. Now new lines had begun to form, ties that bound him slowly but surely to a future that was no longer in his hands. He felt like a trapeze artist bouncing into the net after a failed trick, caught in a spider's web he could no longer escape from, lumbering, ashamed, in a trap of his own making. Perhaps there was still time . . . He could leave some money for Anne at the hotel, jump in the car . . . He could – but already he knew he would not. He was lacking the one small thing that saves a man from drowning, the kick of rage that lifts you up from the bottom and propels you to the surface. It was still a long, long way off. He was not there yet.

'Anne?'

'Yes?'

'Why did you try to get rid of Boudu?'

'What are you talking about? I didn't do anything to your cat. He just went off.'

'There's a pillowcase missing from the cupboard.'

'So? Talk to the chambermaid.'

'Fine. Be like that – but I know it was you.'

'You're really starting to piss me off, you know. And that cat, always hanging around like a bad smell. And purring. Anyway, are you playing?'

Marc laid down his last card, the king of spades.

'Ace of hearts, I win!'

How lost the little red heart looked in the middle of the white rectangle. Anne lit a cigarette and stood before the window, whose glass was thickly tarred by the dark and rainy sky.

'You know you're really bored when you're playing War at six in the evening. Everything's boring in this place. I'd have been better off staying at the hospital.'

'I'll take you back tomorrow if you like.'

'Yes.'

'I'm sorry . . . I would have liked . . . to do something fun with you. Bringing you to Le Touquet at this time of year was never a good idea.'

'It's OK. You always were rubbish at presents.'

'True. I've never had a clue. Tell me what you'd like. If I can . . .'

'Désiré.'

'Désiré . . . the barman?'

'Yes.'

'I think that's beyond me.'

'Like hell it is! Slip him a grand and he'll soon come round.'

'Anne, you can't just buy people like that.'

'Haven't you ever hired a prostitute?'

'No, never.'

'Well then, what do you know?'

'Yes, but this boy isn't a prostitute, he—'

'Wanna bet?'

'Anne, ask me whatever you want, but . . .'

'Forget it. You can take me back tomorrow and we'll never mention this again.'

Anne flopped back onto the bed, lifted up Boudu, who was sleeping on the pillow, and moved his front legs into various positions like some parody of a gymnastic routine. The cat, limp, eyes half shut, was so out of it he did not attempt to put up a fight.

'He's such a wuss, this big stupid cat, you can do whatever you like with him. He's realised the easiest thing is to say yes to everything.'

Of course she had been taking the piss with the Désiré suggestion, but Marc felt frustrated not to be able to offer her anything besides the frivolous pleasures of clothes, haircuts and restaurant meals, which left nothing behind them but a feeling of deep ennui. He had been the one who suggested this trip – she had not asked him to do anything. Of the two of them, it was probably he who was most keenly aware of the void he had opened by taking them on this break.

'Anne, I'm going downstairs for a bit.'

'Yep. See you later.'

There was just one couple at the bar drinking multicoloured cocktails and gazing mournfully at the empty restaurant. Since he had nothing better to do, Désiré was keeping himself busy polishing glasses that didn't need polishing. Seeing Marc, he dropped the act and came over, smiling.

'Evening, Monsieur.'

'Good evening, Désiré. I'll have a scotch, double, no ice.'

'Very good, Monsieur.'

He really was an attractive young man, supple, precise in his movements, neither obsequious nor overly familiar, polite and straightforward.

'There you are, Monsieur. Will Mademoiselle Anne be joining you?'

'For dinner. Tell me, Désiré, what are your plans for this evening?'

'Me? Well, I'm working, up till midnight.'

'And afterwards?'

'Afterwards?'

'Yes.'

'I'm going home. Why?'

'Just wondered.'

Marc downed his drink in one gulp, as Désiré looked on doubtfully.

'Same again.'

'Very good, Monsieur.'

Désiré brought over another glass which followed the same course as the first. Marc almost choked as he finished it. A ball of fire was yoyoing from his head to his toes. It was as if a white-hot iron rod had been plunged into his stomach. The barstool on which he was sitting now seemed twice as high.

'Something wrong, Monsieur?'

'No, no, everything's just fine. Désiré, what do you think of my daughter?'

'Um . . . she's very nice.'

'And?'

'And very . . . simple. I mean, she doesn't put on airs the way a lot of them do around here.'

'Very simple . . . Do you fancy her?'

'Excuse me? I don't understand.'

'Fill me up, please.'

'Of course, coming right up.'

The barstool was getting higher and higher. Soon Marc's head would be brushing the chandelier. Everything around him shone, sparkled and crackled, glowing in the dark like fish in an aquarium. Désiré suddenly reappeared out of nowhere.

'Désiré, I'm going to ask you a favour, nothing more. A . . .'

Marc clutched the bronze bar counter with both hands as he strived to find the word. Where had it gone? There were others pounding his ears like towels against his head, words that were gradually seeping into the aquarium. Bodiless, pointless words, bubbles . . .

'Are you OK, Monsieur?'

'Yes, fine. Do you know Agen?'

'No.'

'It's a lovely town. But it's a long, long way away . . .'

'I'm sure, Monsieur, yes. Excuse me, there are customers.'

Marc grabbed Désire by the wrist, as much to hold him back as to maintain his own precarious balance.

'Would you like to sleep with her tonight?'

'With whom, Monsieur?'

'My daughter.'

Désiré's eyes grew so wide that there was nothing left of his face besides two white saucers with a black olive rolling in the middle. Marc did not let go; his face was close to the barman's.

'This is very important – very! I'll give you five hundred

euros to spend an hour with her after your shift. Don't turn me down – I'm asking as a father!'

Désiré's mouth hung open, as if his bottom jaw had just come loose. Without lowering his gaze, he lifted each of the fingers gripping his arm, one by one.

'Well?'

'I have customers, Monsieur. Please excuse me.'

Marc stayed a while, gazing at his open hand as a strange sense of calm washed over him. All that remained of his drunken state was the serenity of a master who has just freed a slave. The barstool seemed to slide back down to a normal height. He stepped off it without the slightest wobble, and reached the lift, an ineffable smile plastered across his face.

He kept the smile up throughout the meal, during which Anne did not once glance towards the bar or mention Désiré. She seemed to have forgotten him entirely, so absorbed was she in extricating her whelks from their shells.

'Whelks are nice, especially the big ones. What's the matter with your mouth? Are you having a stroke?'

'No.'

'You haven't stopped smiling.'

'That's because I'm happy.'

'It's because you're pissed. You stank of whisky when you came up earlier.'

'Excuse me a minute, I've run out of cigarettes. I'll get some at the bar.'

He had never felt so sure of himself. Everything seemed to have been pre-written, as carefully orchestrated as a musical score.

'Désiré, a pack of Winstons, please.'

As he handed Marc the packet, Désiré blinked slightly. Beneath the cigarettes was a note folded into four: 'OK. But not at the hotel. At mine: 4 Passage Grimaux, third floor, on the left, 12.30. 500 euros.'

Back in the room, when Marc had told Anne she had a date with Désiré at half past midnight, she had simply replied, 'OK,' without looking up from the TV screen, two pillows under her head, Boudu purring on her belly.

It took them a while to find it. All the roads looked the same and the street signs were illegible in the rain. At last Marc pulled up outside a narrow four-storey building and handed Anne the envelope with the five hundred euros.

'Happy?'

'I'll tell you afterwards.'

He watched her, hunched over holding her coat above her head as she crossed the road and vanished into the building, its entrance area suddenly filled with lemon-yellow light. A few minutes later the automatic light clicked off again, returning it to darkness. On the third floor, a bluish light filtered through the shutters.

The rain was pounding the roof of the car, brown ink dripping from the night sky onto the windscreen. A car went by in the other direction with a hiss of tyres, its headlights casting a greenish beam across Marc's dashboard. Marc yawned and stretched his arms. He took his phone out of his pocket. The voicemail was full of messages from Chloé. He picked one at random: 'Marc, where are you? Ple—' He deleted them all. He thought back to the bridge over the motorway and the time she had found him on all fours looking for his childhood in the rug. Where was he? On a road in Le Touquet, at midnight, in the rain, waiting for the daughter he had just paid a Togolese barman to make love to. Everything was fine. Le Touquet was not far, but it was becoming a little further away than before.

Three light knocks on the window woke him with a start. Anne's face came into view like something out of a Bacon portrait. When the door opened, a pocket of air seemed to rush into the car with her.

'OK?'

'Of course I'm OK. Let's go.'

'All right. What's that?'

'A present. A statue from his country, a lucky charm with nails in it.'

The 30cm-high statuette represented a squat little man, his legs slightly bent. His left hand was pressed against his stomach and his right – missing an index finger – open at shoulder height. His jaw was clamped around a metal disc chained to a kind of cannonball between his feet which he seemed to want to wrench from the ground. His head and back, bristling with rusty nails, bowed slightly backwards. The model was made of wood, covered in red clay like coagulated blood, and metal. Its hollow eye sockets stared at Marc, who was sitting on the edge of the bed, unable to take his eyes off it. You could not appraise the statue in the same way as the curiosities Chloé picked up at flea markets, nor even as a work of art. There it was, in the corner of the table, irrefutable, emitting a raw energy that banished all aesthetic considerations. After staring at it for more than an hour, Marc's muscles had hardened so that he seemed to be making as much effort as the little man pulling on his chain.

'Why are you sitting there fully dressed? Didn't you go to bed?'

'Yes, I had a bit of sleep.'

'What time is it?'

'Ten past seven.'

A milky early light seeped through the curtains. Boudu and Anne yawned in unison.

'Can you order breakfast? I've got the *gwamba*.'

'The what?'

'The *gwamba*. I heard about it from Désiré. It's an illness, a kind of fever you get in Africa when you're craving bush meat. It drives you so crazy you'd eat anything, even humans.'

A ray of sunlight lent a glossy sheen to the croissant crumbs strewn across the tray. With deliberate tongue strokes, Boudu ate them one by one, as if he were a mechanical toy. Anne came out of the bathroom, steaming and wrapped in a towelling bathrobe that made her look like a giant spring roll.

'Still no rain?'

'No, I think it's actually going to be a lovely day.'

'It must be weird to see this place in the sunshine.'

'Do you still want to go back to the hospital?'

'I don't know. Yes.'

'Then here's what I suggest. We make the most of the good weather to go for a walk on the beach, have lunch here and then I'll take you back this afternoon.'

'OK.'

Anne bumped into the table on her way past and the statuette wobbled. Marc caught it just in time.

'Don't worry, it's fine.'

'I don't care. It's ugly. Things like that bring bad luck. Look, there's the proof – you've cut yourself on it.'

A drop of blood was forming under Marc's nail.

There were lots of people on the beach, little blots of colour that grew bigger as you drew nearer. It made you wonder where they had come from, these people you saw nowhere else. The sun had probably just conjured them up. Their average age was quite high.

'Must be an open day at the local cemetery.'

Anne seemed sulky. She was taking obvious pleasure in crushing the empty shells under her feet.

'Did it not go well last night?'

'What? With Désiré? No, it went fine. Like a dose of local anaesthetic.'

Marc was put out by Anne's lacklustre response. It had, after all, cost him five hundred euros to get her a shag. And yet he did not regret it. He had paid to dare make it happen, to prove to his daughter that he could meet her strangest whims. Yet clearly he had only succeeded in impressing himself. Still, if it made her feel momentarily better, then why not? What was really bothering him was the thought of going back. Back to what? He had only just left but had already gone too far to turn back. His newfound freedom stood in the way.

'Look, a rat!'

It might have been mistaken for a patch of tar, but was indeed a rat, a dead one, with a bloated stomach, gummed-up fur, stiff paws and a floppy tail, lying on a bed of kelp.

'It must have fallen off a boat.'

'Maybe it came from China?'

'Maybe.'

'All that way just to snuff it at Le Touquet. He'd have been better off staying at home too.'

'Why do you say that?'

'No reason, just saying. For everyone who thinks things are better somewhere else.'

They found two more rats before they reached the lighthouse where they sat to look at the wide-open sea, which at this point on the estuary seemed in fact rather narrow.

'Do you really want to go back to the hospital?'

'Are you going to make me a better offer?'

'Do you know Agen?'

'Agen? Where's that?'

'In the south, the south-west.'

'What's there?'

'Prunes,' he replied without thinking, his head bowed, tracing parallel lines with his toe in the sand.

'Are you constipated?'

'No. I just don't want to go home.'

'Ah.'

There was a boat balancing on the horizon line in the distance, standing almost still.

'Are you not getting on with Chloé?'

'It's not that. I don't want to go back, that's all.'

'So you want to go to Agen.'

'Agen or anywhere, it's all the same to me.'

'But you don't want to go on your own.'

'You don't have to come.'

'Glad to hear it! . . . What are you afraid of?'

'I don't know. Of having regrets.'

'Well then, let's go to Agen. It can't be any worse than this place!'

Having had lunch at the hotel, loaded the luggage in the car and put Boudu on the back seat, Marc asked Anne if she wanted to say goodbye to Désiré.

'What for?'

He said nothing. Anyway, while settling the bill at reception, he had learned that Désiré had not shown up for work that morning. There was another barman standing in for him, a tall redhead riddled with freckles.

'I don't believe in the dead.'

'The dead? What do you mean?'

'They don't exist.'

'Death doesn't exist?'

'No, "the dead", people dying.'

'Why do you say that?'

'Listening to this news on the radio. This guy they're talking about from the Académie Française – I don't think he's dead. Nor are the ones from the air accident or the terror attack in Egypt. They can say what they like, show us pictures on telly. It's not true.'

'No?'

'No. They take people to one side, give them a new face and identity, and they go on living on islands far away. No one's ever really dead.'

'And why would "they" do that?'

'To scare us. To give us a good reason to live.'

'And who are "they"?'

'I don't know. Staff. I've had enough of their nonsense. I'm putting some music on.'

Anne started fiddling with the car radio, setting off a stream of jumbled frequencies, broken sentences and bursts of song. Still unsatisfied, she switched it off.

As the sun went down, the countryside rolled by like a naïve painting of valleys, clumps of trees, hamlets of houses clinging together to keep warm, yellow lights in windows and ribbons of smoke curling up from chimneys. Marc yawned and stretched, his arms taut on the steering wheel. Dusk had always made him want to go indoors and curl up in front of the fire. To be inside one of the houses they were passing, hearing snatches of trivial chitchat and smelling soup on the stove, would have filled him with happiness. Every so often he felt an irritating itch coming from the finger he had caught on one of the nails sticking out of the doll. It wasn't painful but might become so. He would go to the pharmacist tomorrow. He switched on the headlights, catching a sign saying 'Limoges 20 km' in their beam.

'I'm feeling a bit tired. Shall we stop in Limoges for the night?'

All towns are grey by night and Limoges was no exception. They could have been anywhere. Thanks to a big international conference in town, the only hotel they could find was a grotty place on the outskirts. Their window looked out on a ring road cutting through the retail park whose neon lights gave the sky a bilious green tinge. Pale puffy clouds floated above like the bellies of whales. They had to make do with floppy pizzas for dinner, bought from a van the hotel receptionist had pointed them towards. Marc had barely managed a quarter of his.

'Aren't you hungry?'

'Not very.'

'Can I finish it?'

'Go ahead.'

The window was shut but the roar of passing lorries made the bedroom walls shake. A nearby stop sign forced vehicles to brake and then move off again, wheezing and puffing like angry bulls. The noise came in waves, almost in time with the shooting pains in Marc's finger. As bizarre as it was, it gave him a kind of thrill, as if he were the one directing the on-off throbbing. Lying on the bed with his eyes closed, he let the waves swell and crash down again, each one causing a little more damage than the last.

'You're quiet.'

'I'm tired. And my finger's bothering me.'

'Show me.'

Marc held out his index finger. It was red and swollen, with a white spot under the nail.

'Does it hurt?'

'A bit. I'll go to the pharmacist tomorrow.'

Anne returned his hand to him, making a face.

'You should, yeah. You ought to have it cut off.'

'That might be going a bit far.'

'I'm saying it for your own good, I don't care. It's your own fault – you shouldn't have touched the stupid doll.'

'It's nothing. I'll go and see a doctor, he'll give me a tetanus jab and that'll be the end of it.'

'Doctors can't treat that kind of thing. You need to get it cut off.'

'Anne, I pricked my finger. You don't die from a scratch.'

'You could, but you'll rot first. Last year I had an abscess in one of my molars. I would rather have died a hundred times over. It's stupid being in pain, and pointless. They took my tooth out and I was all right again. Get your finger cut off and that'll be that. Anything that hurts just needs cutting off.'

The bed creaked as she stood up. Boudu was licking the pizza boxes. Anne ruffled his head.

'Useful, this cat. You can lug him from place to place and he never kicks up a fuss. He just needs a handle to carry him with. I'm still hungry too. Fancy a crêpe? The pizza guy sells them.'

'No, thanks. But if you could ask for an aspirin at reception . . .'

Boudu accompanied Anne to the door with his tail in the air and once she had closed it behind her, leapt up onto Marc's stomach which he began pawing as he purred away, eyes half shut. Stay still, stay still.

Marc woke with a start, sending Boudu flying to the end of the bed where, after a few seconds of uncertainty, he became absorbed in a thorough cleaning operation in an attempt to appear unruffled. Anne was still not back. The red numbers on the clock radio showed 4.10 a.m. What crazy dream had he just woken up from? He was taking a bath . . . yes, that was it, he was lathering himself up. Through the window, he was watching uniformed police officers digging up his lawn. They were looking for bodies, bodies that he, Marc, had buried. He knew he was guilty – he wasn't denying it. Yet it was not the certainty of being arrested and sent to prison that bothered him, but the fact he could no longer remember whom he had killed, nor why, nor when.

As he made his way into the bathroom for a drink of water, he caught the impenetrable gaze of the doll standing next to the greasy pizza boxes. He couldn't remember taking it out of the luggage. Had Anne? Under the bright ceiling light, the nail-studded talisman seemed to thrum feverishly, as painful to look at as the filament in a light bulb. Marc threw the contents of the tooth glass over it and immediately regretted it, as if he had just committed some sacrilegious act. Yet no lightning came to strike him down, and he went peacefully back to sleep as if without a care in the world.

'You were back late.'

'Oh. Maybe.'

'I woke up around four and you weren't here.'

'I went for a walk. I couldn't sleep. Shall we go?'

The hotel lobby felt like a fish tank. The receptionist and a chambermaid had their noses pressed to the glass entrance. Flashing blue lights from outside swept across the walls and ceiling.

'What's going on?'

'The pizza van burned down. The guy was inside it.'

'Is he . . .?'

'Yes. Will you be having breakfast?'

'No, thank you. Do you know of any doctors nearby?'

'A doctor, round here? You could try Dr Blanchard on Avenue Foch, but I don't know if he's still practising. Turn left at the second roundabout heading back towards the town centre, where they're building the new stadium. You can't miss it – it's the only house still standing.'

At the car park exit, a police officer held them back to let an ambulance screech out onto the ring road ahead of them, sirens blazing. All that remained of the pizza van was a charred, smoking carcass with police and firefighters swarming around it. Marc remembered the baby-faced *pizzaiolo*.

'He was young, the pizza guy.'

'Served him right. His pizzas were disgusting.'

Avenue Foch was nothing more than a giant building site, a no man's land strewn with rubble and bent metal girders in which a detached millstone house stood miraculously unscathed, a strange vestige of a distant past. A greening copper doorplate testified to the occupant's noble profession: P. Blanchard, Doctor of Medicine. So Marc hoped. He rang the bell. Cranes wheeled and screeched in the sulphurous yellow sky as enormous machines belched, combing the earth with their steel teeth. Holes, heaps, heaps of holes. Marc had to shout into the intercom to make himself heard. Even with the door closed behind them, the din of the building site shook the walls of the house from the cellar up to the attic. A wash of grey light trickled through the frosted glass window at the top of the narrow, steep staircase. A croaky voice invited them to come up.

Even if you hooked a finger under his chin and lifted it, Dr Blanchard could not have been taller than 5'2". He was old enough to be ageless and, despite being swamped in countless layers of dubious woollens, looked impossibly thin. His left eye squinted up at you aslant, while the right eye, veiled with an opaque spot, ignored you entirely.

'. . . in . . . down.'

Marc and Anne sat down on two worn velvet armchairs covered in cat hair. A strong smell of urine, though overlain with ether, confirmed the constant presence of a feline. The doctor's good eye immediately fell on Anne.

'How many weeks?'

Anne turned to her father, eyebrows arched in query. Marc cut in.

'Excuse me, doctor, but we're here for me.'

'Oh.'

From then on, the doctor accorded Anne no more attention than the profound disdain of his dead eye.

'What's the matter with you?'

'Practically nothing. I pricked my finger on a rusty nail and—'

'Show me.'

Somewhat reluctantly, Marc gave up his hand to the dry claw of the doctor, who whistled like a punctured balloon as he leaned over it.

'Not a pretty sight! When did it happen?'

'The day before yesterday.'

'A rusty nail, you said?'

'Yes. On an African talisman.'

'Ah, I see! . . . Just as I thought . . . I know Africa, you see! Just take a look at the souvenir I got from there.'

Craning his tortoise-like neck over his desk, he offered Marc the unappetising sight of his cloudy eye.

'Pus spurted right into it while I was operating on a bubo

as putrid as your finger. I'll bet your rotten old talisman came from Benin, or maybe Togo, am I right?'

'From Togo, I think.'

'Well, there you go! It's some kind of voodoo black-magic business. How do you expect medicine to help? It's not looking good for you, Monsieur, not good at all. Oh, for Christ's sake, I've had it with these people!'

The window behind him had just swung open with a thud, to the sound of falling scree. The doctor flung himself against the railing.

'Bastards! Bunch of arseholes! You won't get me, by God, you won't! I'm indestructible, do you hear me? I'll destroy you, I don't care how many of you there are. Twenty years in Africa and I lived to tell the tale! Blanchard's still standing, you pieces of shit!'

Shaking with rage, he closed the window and returned to his seat opposite Marc and Anne, looking them up and down as if he had only just set eyes on them.

'Right, where were we? Either we cut it off, or else there's nothing I can do. Up to you. I'll do the amputation for 100 euros. That's a good price.'

Marc looked expectantly at his finger as if it might make the decision for him.

'What if I keep my finger?'

'Then you'll begin to rot a little more each day. First your hand, then your forearm, up to your shoulder, all the way to your heart. It might take a fortnight, a month or a year. Depends on your constitution. But you'll rot either way.'

'I . . . I'll think about it.'

'As you wish. That'll be twenty-five euros.'

Outside, it looked as if it had been snowing. The car was covered in a fine sprinkling of white dust. Nearby a chair on a patch of flooring was precariously balanced against a half-collapsed wall covered in peeling wallpaper.

Marc was sitting on a tree stump soaking his finger in a cup of disinfectant solution bought from a pharmacy in a small town just outside Cahors. It was so warm they had decided to have a picnic by the river. It was a delightful spot. Polystyrene debris floated by on the current, Anne was spreading truffle foie gras onto thick slices of bread and, in the distance, a chainsaw could be heard topping acres of forest. After the Dr Blanchard incident, Marc had resolved if not to recover, at least put an end to his suffering. He had achieved this by taking three paracetamol and numbing the finger in this liquid, which smelled reassuringly of a Swiss toilet.

'This is nice, isn't it?'

'Yes, not bad.'

'You know, if I lived here, I'd buy a fishing rod. I'd get up early and come and sit here quietly, dipping my line in the water . . .'

'And the chainsaw-carrying lunatic would jump out of a bush and cut your throat just to get the watch off your wrist.'

'Why would you say that?'

'Because peaceful little spots don't exist, especially not in the countryside.'

'You see the bad in everything.'

'For good reason. More pâté?'

'It's foie gras, Anne. Foie gras, not pâté. Hey, listen . . . the chainsaw's stopped.'

'Then the madman's clocked us.'

Marc shrugged, but deep down he had to admit there was something disconcerting about this sudden silence, broken only by the birds whose chirruping could again be heard. Anne snorted with her mouth full.

'I was joking. Hey, don't you think it might be time for a new car?'

'Why? This one works perfectly well.'

'That's not the problem. Surely it's crossed your mind Chloé hasn't just been twiddling her thumbs since you upped and left. She'll have reported you missing. We'll hit a roadblock and bam, it's game over. Plus it's an ugly old banger, I never could stand it. It smells.'

Marc thought about this for a moment. Anne was not wrong. Knowing Chloé as he did, there was no doubt in his mind that she would have taken steps to find him. Yet he had nothing to feel guilty about. He hadn't broken the law; it was a private matter. But the idea of having to explain himself to the authorities and, worse, to his spouse, even just on the phone, was too much to contemplate. Getting a new car wasn't such a bad idea. It was Chloé who had chosen this one: 'You can always trust a German car'; if it had been up to him, he'd have gone for a British or Italian make. Something with a bit more class.

'Well, why not?'

A few hours later, after protracted negotiations with a dealer, they left the outskirts of Cahors at the wheel of a barely used camper van as handsome as a refrigerator truck.

They stopped for their first night in the camper van outside the little village of Laugnac, twenty or so kilometres from Agen. Anne was as excited as when she was a little girl opening her presents on Christmas morning.

'Bit of a step up from your old-man wagon, you have to admit.'

'It's nice, yes.'

'We're at home wherever we go! Tired? You can go to sleep. Hungry? Have something to eat. Fridge, hob – it's got everything! What else could you ask for? Look how happy Boudu is!'

Curled up in the corner of the bed, the cat's fluffy tail beat to the gentle rhythm of his purrs.

'No more grovelling waiters, no shitty Van Gogh prints on the walls, no thank you, hello, goodbye, we don't owe anything to anyone. More soup?'

'No, thanks. It was lovely.'

'Go and give your finger a soak outside then while I make the bed. We'll be snug as bugs in a rug!'

The pharmacist had advised him to repeat the procedure three times a day for three days. If, as he feared, his finger showed no sign of improvement, then he could go to see a specialist. Perching on the edge of the step with the cup wedged between his knees, Marc watched the flickering, graceful curve of an aeroplane crossing a field of scattered stars. How could he be rotting to death under a sky like that? That crazy Dr Blanchard had put the wind up him, but he was nuts, a decrepit old thing turned mad by malaria or some other fever. The pharmacist, buttoned up in his neatly ironed white coat, had merely diagnosed a harmless inflammation, not even whitlow. And he was clearly right. What was more, it was barely a year since his last tetanus injection (having scraped himself helping Chloé change the knob on one of her nightstands), which would guard him against complications. Voodoo? Yeah, right. Savage superstition. A nail is a nail, Togolese or otherwise. As for the stupid talisman, he would throw it in the nearest tip tomorrow and that would be the end of it. He now felt perfectly serene and confident, in complete symbiosis with the vast night sky surrounding him, the resounding clang of the village bell striking ten times and the distant barking of a dog pulling on its lead. He stood up and went to empty the contents of the cup onto a tuft of dandelions, which immediately withered like an old lettuce heart forgotten in the bottom of the fridge. His camper van really was a thing of beauty. It was Anne who had encouraged him to choose it. He would never have dared go for something like this by himself, yet it was exactly what he needed. A set of wheels like this could take him to the end of the world. It gave him a feeling of invincibility that made the prospect of adventure undaunting. Nothing seemed beyond reach now, the proof being that Agen was now only twenty-two kilometres away. Not that he gave a toss about Agen now. He had far more exotic destinations in his sights, and he wouldn't be holding back!

Had he really slept? With Boudu weighing on his head like a hot-water bottle, Anne occupying three quarters of the bed and the pair of them snoring loudly, he felt as if he had navigated the night on stepping stones, jumping from one absurd dream to another. At the first light of dawn he had emerged, dazed, from the igloo on wheels, hoping for some miracle to bring him back down to earth – earth which was spongy beneath his feet, sticky with dew as if a feverish sweat clung to it. The bell chimed eight times, setting off a commotion that rocked the van as if a mud-flinging contest were going on inside. Anne's face, still puffy with sleep, appeared in the doorway.

'You're up already? If it wasn't for the fucking bell, I'd still be asleep. Coffee?'

'I'm going into the village. Need to stretch my legs. Want me to get you anything?'

'Cigarettes.'

It was a bright, chilly morning. Each little house had a small garden laid out in front of it like a grandmother's apron filled with flowers and fruits. Energetic octogenarians in blue

83

cotton slacks and rubber clogs were already out digging and pruning their little plots, nodding in response to the jovial greeting Marc called out on his way past. It made you want to be old, to have reached the end of everything, to dig your hole and lie in it happily, telling yourself, 'It may be little, but it's home.' 'The right hole' was exactly what he found at the café-tobacconist-grocer-breadstore Au Bon Trou, chez Maurice and Tinette, which he entered, causing a bell to ring and Maurice (it couldn't be Tinette with that Gallic moustache) and three natives at the bar to shoot stares at him. It was as warm and yellow as egg yolk inside. Marc took a seat at a table and rubbed his hands together.

'A large coffee, please, and some bread and jam if you've got it.'

To entertain himself, he started to read a rag picked up from a neighbouring table. Despite the abundant facial hair, the glimpse Marc caught of a support stocking informed him just in time that the person bringing the coffee and bread was Tinette and not Maurice, saving him from committing a terrible faux pas.

'Thank you, Madame.'

Judging by the events that filled the news-in-brief pages, this was a sleepy sort of area: car accidents (mostly involving young drivers who had got their licences only months before), the theft of a widow's bathroom sink, a row over cockerels and church bells. Nothing of any importance. News from paradise, you might say.

The bread was as bad as could be found in any supermarket,

but at least the coffee was hot. From time to time, the bell tinkled as other customers entered, tall, fat, small, thin, young and old, buying cigarettes, a magazine or bread, exchanging banal comments with Tinette about the weather or such-and-such's health. Life in paradise. This was precisely how Marc saw it: insignificance taken to perfection. No one paid attention to him, as if he were invisible. As he melted into the warm, bovine atmosphere, he undressed his fellow customers with his eyes, peeling off their outer skins one by one, stripping them from head to foot, revealing them as God made them with their crooked, hairy legs and varicose veins, impressive rolls of pale flesh amassed around their guts, wormy blue veins wiggling up their arms, calves covered in shrivelled flesh, or taut enough to snap, flab, bones, fat, spots, vaccination scars, war wounds, moles, warts, hollow chests appearing empty of breath, others bursting with suppressed cries, hard nipples and nipples drooping sadly from empty, crumpled saddlebags, fanned, semi-webbed toes, and toes squashed together in narrow high heels, stranglers' hands with knobbly fingers, hard as tools, fingers of church saints, as long and pale as candles. A full-on striptease: incredible!

Having got on to the topic of fingers, he inevitably remembered his own, which he contemplated with a look of bafflement as he rested his elbow on the table. He was not in pain, but the index finger was still just as swollen and had turned a strange orange colour which he put down to the product in which he was marinating it three times a day.

'Was there something else you wanted?'

Marc jumped. His finger, held in the air like a schoolboy asking permission to speak, had caught Tinette's attention.

'No . . . umm, what do I owe you?'

The return leg always feels shorter than the way out. It's because you know where you're going. Marc already had his bearings – there was the little house with blue shutters, the farming co-op, the collapsed wall . . . He felt at home here. Only, his home appeared to have vanished. In the spot where the camper van had been parked, there were now only tyre tracks veering from the grass onto the tarmac of the road towards Agen.

Even though he was alone, Marc said aloud the last word we all resort to at times of extreme disarray: 'Shit!'

His immediate response was to sit down. But there was nothing, not a rock or a tree stump, still less a bench or handy Voltaire chair to settle into. So instead, with arms hanging by his sides, he walked several times round the perimeter of the patch of yellowed grass where barely an hour ago his camper van had stood. The interesting thing about the last word is that it isn't the last word at all, but can be multiplied at leisure to fill the void of an unsolvable enigma. Which he did, in a range of tones of voice, like an actor rehearsing lines. Then, trying to regain control of the situation, he began constructing a series of hypotheses to find a semblance of sense where apparently there was none. Anne had been attacked . . . by a prowler . . . gypsies . . . She had been kidnapped, raped . . . Knowing his daughter, this seemed unlikely. She had been killed, then, strangled, stabbed and thrown into a ditch, a ditch so thick with brambles it was impenetrable. And Boudu? What had they done with him? Was he still in the camper van or huddled against the mutilated body of his mistress?

Having armed himself with a stick, Marc was beginning to beat back brambles, muttering 'Boudu? . . . Boudu?' when the familiar sound of a diesel engine caught his attention. Anne drew into the exact spot the van had occupied an hour earlier. She was not alone – a young man resembling a baby ostrich, his long neck emerging from a loose polo neck jumper, was sitting beside her.

'Anne!'

'What on earth are you doing with that stick? Looking for snails?'

'Anne, where were you?'

'I went for a drive. I wanted to give it a spin. It's great.'

'But you don't have a licence. You—'

'Who gives a toss? I know how to drive. Oh, this is Zoltan. He's Hungarian.'

Anne gestured to the slender Magyar who unfolded his six-foot frame and marched purposefully towards Marc, a carnival smile hanging from his sticking-out ears.

'I Zoltan, Hungaria.'

Marc shook the cold, bony outstretched hand, wondering how they were going to deal with this.

'Anne, where's he going?'

'No idea. He hardly speaks a word of French. He was hitching, I picked him up. He seems nice, doesn't he?'

It was true, he didn't seem aggressive. He carried his village-idiot grin with as much conviction as his huge red rucksack, gazing enthusiastically at everything around him – the trees, the sky, the camper van, Anne, Marc and the village bell tower.

It had nothing to do with his finger, although it did now have the turgescent appearance of a freshly dug carrot. No, this time it was his legs. They had simply refused to obey him when he tried to stand up from the step and dust the crumbs of his sandwich off his lap. No pain, pins and needles or cramp. His legs had simply gone on strike, without prior warning. The rest of his body — the torso, arms, neck, head — continued to work perfectly. Marc had been reduced to a torso as Anne, munching a slice of ham, looked on in bafflement, as did Zoltan, who could not tell if Marc's vain attempts to stand up were part of some weird after-dinner ritual. Anne swallowed the ribbon of fat and rind she always saved until last.

'What the hell are you doing jiggling around like that?'

'It's my legs.'

'What about them?'

'It's ridiculous. I can't get them to move.'

'Oh. Wait a bit, maybe you'll get the feeling back.'

'Maybe . . . they're not hurting. See, everything down to my middle is fine.'

Marc was swinging his arms from left to right and turning his head from side to side, so that everyone could see for themselves how perfectly the top half of his body moved. Zoltan, convinced he was indeed witnessing a local custom, took it upon himself to begin imitating Marc, throwing his arms wide and moving them about with a grin that showed all his teeth, which were as yellow as a donkey's and wide as spades. Marc immediately ceased his grotesque choreography.

Anne was picking her teeth, looking uncertain.

'So we're not going to Agen?'

'It doesn't seem likely at the moment. Maybe I should have a lie-down on the bed?'

'Maybe . . . Do we have to carry you?'

'Well, yes, I'm afraid you might have to.'

'Zoltan!'

With Anne holding him under the arms and the Hungarian under the knees, Marc let himself be hauled into the camper van like a piece of furniture and left lying in the foetal position in the middle of the bed.

'Thanks. We'll just have to wait a while.'

'If you need anything, I'll be outside.'

'OK, Anne . . . What is it? Why are you looking at me like that?'

'You're all red. You look like the doll, curled up, waving your finger in the air. See you later.'

He couldn't lie on his back or front, but he could switch from side to side. If he chose his left, his gaze confronted the wall of the vehicle; his right, the white expanse of the fridge door. His immediate future held no prospect of more distant horizons. In the course of Marc's installation, Boudu had allowed himself to be moved to the foot of the bed without in any way abandoning his constant search for perfection.

His purring sounded like a wood-burning stove. Anne and Zoltan's muffled voices reached Marc's ears, repeated words, bursts of laughter . . . She must be teaching him some basic French. A tractor passed by and he listened to the engine gradually revving up and then slowing again.

'Life without me . . .'

There was a scratch at the bottom of the fridge door as if someone had angrily kicked it shut. The grim grey carpet was almost threadbare in one area. A stain in the shape of Spain had been rubbed at too vigorously. What had happened here? A drunken evening? To celebrate buying the camper van, perhaps . . . Yes, this place had a past. People had eaten, drunk, slept, made plans, lost illusions, loved one another – here, on this bed. What had led them to sell the camper van only six months after they bought it? The vehicle raised so many questions it was worthy of paleontological study, like a modern-day Lascaux which Marc was discovering, face to face with the traces of the previous inhabitants of this destabilising black hole. People like him, like anyone, like the ones he had undressed with his eyes this morning at the café, Tinettes . . . What traces would he leave behind? Tyre tracks . . . People like him, like anyone . . .

'No! Not like me! Not like me!!'

Anne's face appeared in the doorway.

'What's going on? Why are you shouting?'

'It's nothing. I was drifting off. I had a nightmare.'

'Oh right. I'm going for a walk with Zoltan. Legs still not right?'

'No, but I'm fine. See you later.'

He had shouted 'Not like me!' just as he had blurted 'I know Agen, too!' at the dinner party two months ago, so that for just one moment he could feel he existed: 'Not like me!' But what made him any different from other people? Precisely the fact that they were other people and he was himself, the one and only Marc Lecas, and if he was no more, then other people – each and every one of them – would disappear with him, because their existence depended wholly on his. After Marc Lecas there would be nothing, zero, an empty car park, a beach without footsteps in the sand, a cloudless sky, a gaping chasm of nothingness. There would be nobody left . . . The enormity of this revelation propelled him to interstellar heights and he was just preparing to blow himself into outer space when a searing electric shock tore through his finger. The pain was bringing him back to life, but it was not a pretty sight. There was something obscene about the purplish, erectile index finger topped with its black nail. A probing, threatening, accusatory finger that might cause whatever it pointed at to wither and die. And now that the burning sensation was becoming truly intolerable, the finger was becoming an even greater burden, as every second that passed brought a new wave of white heat. It was enough to drive you crazy, like a ticking time bomb, tick, tock . . . If he'd had an axe within reach, Marc would not have hesitated to use it. But there was none. So he opened the fridge and plunged his hand into the ice tray.

Lying right on the edge of the bed with his arm outstretched was not the most comfortable position, but the relief that came in contact with the ice largely made up for it.

It was perfectly possible to do without your right index finger. It was perfectly possible to do without all kinds of things. Other than the head and the heart, most things were not essential. But still, he wasn't going to spend his life with his hand in a fridge. He must make a firm, definite decision as quickly as possible. He remembered a kidnapping that had been all over the news. The kidnappers had cut off the finger of their victim, a well-known businessman who, when asked about the incident after his release, could only recall a clean, almost painless cut. A good knife and bam! Over and done with. Only, in Marc's case, who would wield the knife? Not him, because he was right-handed and that was the hand he couldn't use. Anne? . . . She would certainly be capable of it . . . on the board they used to slice *saucisson* . . . he would just have to close his eyes . . . bam! A clean, precise blow, like the butcher slicing up chops. 'Will that be all, Madame?' As simple as a trip to the butcher's. And when it was done, they would never speak of it again.

'Anne . . .? Anne?'

No answer. Oh, yes, she had gone for a walk with Zoltan. What was that guy doing here? Trust Anne to find a Hungarian on the outskirts of Agen. Although they were probably to be found elsewhere too. Sooner or later a Zoltan always makes his way into your life, just when you've made up your mind to have your finger amputated by your daughter.

The clock radio had come on. They were talking about a crewed space mission, gushing over the courage of the astronauts spinning at a dizzying 450 kilometres above our heads. It was the same distance from Paris to Limoges – nothing to write home about. Marc had long since sailed higher. He was cold, as if someone had slid a pane of glass down his back. Apart from the line of light trickling from the part-open fridge, it was dark inside the van. His hand was still in the ice tray but his arm was paralysed all the way up to the shoulder. He had been sleeping so well. What did he care about these explorers of the lunar suburbs? He was much further away, much more alone . . . He was overwhelmed by such a deep sense of abandonment that he had to bury his left fist in his mouth to stop himself crying out in terror. Just then, the camper van began to list and the door swung open.

'Anne!'

'It's freezing. What are you doing in the fridge? Are you hungry?'

'No, I was in pain. My finger.'

'And your legs?'

'I don't know. It's my finger . . .'

'Mind out. I've done some shopping. I need to put it away.'

'Is Zoltan not with you?'

'No, he'd had enough. He went to Agen.'

Marc rolled onto his right side, his hand and arm to all intents and purposes fossilised. The Hungarian's absence was altogether good news. The act he was about to ask his daughter to carry out did not require the presence of a third party.

'I got cassoulet, cheese, rum and lemon to make hot toddy. Next time we should stop at a campsite so we can hook up to the electricity rather than run off the battery. We could get a little telly as well, couldn't we? The two of us will be bored shitless in the evenings otherwise.'

'Anne, I need to ask you something.'

'What?'

'I have to have my finger cut off.'

'Do you want to go to hospital?'

'No. It has to be done here, now.'

'And who's going to do it?'

'You.'

'Me . . .? Right now? Before dinner?'

'I'm serious, Anne. Look, it's gone all black. The gangrene will spread. We can't wait any longer. I'm ready.'

'Couldn't you have asked the old git in Limoges?'

'I was scared. I thought it would be OK. You know you can do it.'

'With what? The bread knife?'

'Yes. On the chopping board. One clean blow . . .'

'You've got a nerve asking me . . .'

'It's a matter of life or death.'

'It's a matter of pissing me off!'

She lit the gas lamp with a sigh and took his hand. Sitting in the ring of white light, she had something of the fortune teller in a gypsy caravan.

'We could cut it at the first knuckle. You'd still have a bit of finger left.'

'Do whatever you think. Just be quick.'

He immediately regretted what he had just said. Anne had picked up the board and the knife, clutching his hand firmly between her knees. He had not expected her to make up her mind so quickly. 'Be quick' was a figure of speech, like 'Just a minute, Mr Executioner.' But Anne was a woman of action, she acted first and thought about it afterwards, if she thought about it at all. Her knife-wielding shadow loomed terrifyingly behind her.

'Anne, wait!'

'What?'

'I don't know . . . Give me some rum.'

'You're such a pain in the arse! Do you want this to take all night?'

She poured him a glass, all the while muttering about how hungry and cold and tired she was and how now was really not the time and a whole lot of other things he didn't catch because the drink had set off a violent coughing fit. Having caught sight of the chopping board and the long knife, sacred objects generally used to cut food from which he would be offered scraps, Boudu had come to join them.

'Right, ready? I'll count to three. One . . .'

Neither two, nor three. It was the noise that hurt the most. The same crack you heard when you struck a bit of cartilage in a veal chop. Other than that it was just cold, an intensely cold sensation that paralysed him from head to foot. His jaws seemed welded to one another and his eyelids forever sewn shut on a vision of the past.

'Shit, the blood's pouring out! We'll have to cauterise it.'

'Just a bandage. A bit of alcohol to disinfect it and a bandage.'

'And you think I've got all that stuff with me? It's not as if I was planning on doing an operation this evening. I'm telling you, we need to cauterise it. Wait, I've got an idea.'

Anne went to the front of the van and searched the dashboard. She was like a giant striding about inside a matchbox. Marc's face was glazed with cold sweat. The hostage was right, you hardly felt anything, maybe just a lack . . . After a minute, Anne reappeared holding something in her hand that was glowing like embers.

'What's that?'

'The cigarette lighter. Don't move, it's the perfect fit.'

The burn was so sharp and so sudden he didn't hear himself scream before losing consciousness.

Anne and Boudu were sharing a tin of sardines when Marc resurfaced. It was light outside. The pain in his right hand, wrapped in a towel, had dulled slightly, leaving a vague heat like a fire smouldering under ash. He realised he could now move his legs. His mouth was coated, caramel-like, with the taste of rum. He would have given anything for a big cup of coffee at Tinette's café. It was freezing. Anne was wearing her coat and hat. Everything around him looked messy and dirty. How had they come to live like tramps so quickly? Open tins of food, crusts of bread, orange peel, dirty glasses, various food wrappers . . . and a smell like an upturned dustbin, like burnt flesh . . .

'Ah, you're awake. How are you feeling?'

'It stinks in here. Can you open the door, please?'

'You must be joking. It's freezing outside. How's your hand?'

'It's OK.'

'You've found your feet again, at least. You gave me a bloody great kick before you keeled over, you bastard. Want a coffee?'

'Yes . . . No, not here, it smells too bad. In the village.'

'Will you be all right to get there?'

'I think so. Anne, what did you do with my finger?'

'The fingertip?'

'Yes.'

'I don't know. It must still be on the chopping board . . . Wait . . . yes, it's there.'

'That's what stinks. We need to bury it. Then we can go to the café. Help me up.'

Pissing with one hand is not easy, especially when you're still wobbly on your feet. The pale rays of sunlight were beginning to melt the duvet of white ice covering the bramble leaves. Little by little, Marc began to feel more sure of himself. Anne was waiting behind him holding the chopping board and something which could have passed for an old piece of chorizo.

'Where shall we bury it then?'

Marc scanned the ground around him. 'Anywhere' is not an easy place to pinpoint. He felt as if he were on a beach trying to choose where to lay his towel.

'Are you going to make up your mind?'

'There.'

Marc pointed to a random tuft of grass on the embankment. Anne was about to pull it up when he stopped her.

'No, not there. It's too close to the road. Everyone will drive over it.'

'So?'

'That won't work. It's a piece of me, after all . . . Imagine the tractors . . . We need to find somewhere more suitable.'

'Shall I make you a little marble mausoleum to put it in, with your name in gold letters? It's just a piece of rotten meat. Make your mind up, or I'll throw it into the bushes.'

'You wouldn't, would you?'

'Watch me!'

Before Marc could grab her arm to stop her, using the chopping board as a racquet she had sent the defunct index finger flying over the brambles into the bottom of the ditch, where it bounced off something big and red. Marc was open-mouthed.

'You did it!'

'Good riddance. Things like that attract animals. Don't go off looking for it. In a few hours there'll be nothing left of your sodding finger to play knucklebones with. Now, are we going to have this coffee?'

Despite his annoyance at the lack of solemn funeral rites, Marc took comfort in retracing the familiar route to Au Bon Trou: the house with the blue shutters, the collapsed wall, the farming co-op . . . Everything was getting back to normal. The tinkling of the bell as he pushed open the café door made him feel he was entering paradise. Yet, as they sat down at their table, Marc became aware of some commotion at the bar. Those who had yesterday sat peacefully sipping their drinks, clinging to the counter like mussels, now seemed to be in the grips of a kind of fever, brows furrowed, frowning, exchanging onomatopoeia thick with innuendo. The inscrutable Tinette came to take their order. She had changed her blouse but not her moustache.

'What's going on?' Marc asked tentatively.

'A dead body.'

'A dead body?'

'A Hungarian, so it seems. He was found this morning on the Agen road with his head smashed in.'

'A Hungarian?'

'So they're saying. If you ask me, Hungarians . . . So, two large coffees and some bread and jam.'

Anne chewed in silence, indifferent to the kerfuffle around her. She flicked idly through a copy of the previous day's paper, the one filled with mundane news items, whose pages were not yet haunted by a Hungarian corpse. There couldn't be dozens and dozens of Hungarians in this area. Marc's thoughts had, of course, immediately turned to Zoltan, and thus also to his daughter, who, if it really was him, had surely been one of the last to see him alive.

'Anne, do you think it's Zoltan?'

'Who?'

'The dead Hungarian.'

'How should I know? . . . It's dangerous, hitchhiking.'

After her terse response, Marc paid for their breakfasts and they headed back to the camper van without exchanging a word. On their return, Anne offered to let Marc stay outside to have a cigarette while she cleaned up. Marc wandered towards the bushes where Anne had chucked his finger. The branches had been trampled here. The big red object was still lying in the bottom of the ditch. It looked like a kind of nylon bag . . . A rucksack.

They arrived in Agen around two. Marc parked by the covered market, where half a dozen road sweepers were cleaning up the remnants of the morning's activities. Rotten cabbages, carrots, potatoes and lettuces filled crates stacked in fragile pyramids. The sky was overcast, as if covered by a milky substance of an almost pearl-grey colour. Apart from the staff dressed in green and yellow, everything was grey.

'So this is Agen?'

Marc didn't answer. Of course this wasn't Agen. It couldn't be. They had passed Agen long ago. Now they were simply somewhere else, where the estuary of far, far away opens out into an ocean of possibilities. Anne wound down her window to flick away her cigarette butt.

'What are we doing now?'

'All I know is there's no going back.'

'Why not? If we're not going anywhere else, I may as well go back to the hospital.'

'And act like nothing's happened?'

'Exactly. Anyway, what has happened?'

'Oh, nothing much. Désiré, the pizza guy, Zoltan . . .'

'What are you talking about? What do those three have to do with anything?'

'What "did" they have to do with anything?'

'I don't get it. If you want to carry on talking rubbish, go ahead, but I'm going for a walk.'

'Anne, I saw Zoltan's rucksack in the ditch.'

'He must have chucked it. He wanted to travel light.'

'Anne, please, stop! I'm not judging you. I'm not even asking why you did it. I know now, that's all. I'm with you, I want to protect you, help you . . . We have to think about tomorrow . . .'

They sat for some time watching the dustbin lorries chewing up and swallowing heaps of rubbish. The floors of the covered market were being sluiced, leaving them shining like a skating rink. Anne closed her eyes and sighed, bending her neck against the headrest.

'It wears me out, thinking about tomorrow, or even later today. I never could. We can go wherever you like, it doesn't matter.'

'It's my fault. I should never have dragged you into this. I was only thinking of myself.'

'Me, me, me! Go and die if you feel so guilty about it! Or else . . . let's go to Spain.'

'Spain?'

'Well, yeah. It's not very far.'

'And what'll we do in Spain?'

'The same as in Agen.'

'Give me the map.'

The garage smelled of hot rubber and engine oil. Here and there, the sounds of hammer blows and clinking chains and pulleys rang out beneath the glass roof. The mechanic gave the tyre on the camper van one last kick and turned to Marc, wiping his hands with a greasy cloth.

'Needs a new engine.'

'Excuse me?'

'It's had it. The rest of it's all right, but . . . needs a new engine.'

'Can you do it?'

''Course we can, but with all the work we've got on, we're talking at least a week's wait.'

'A week!'

'Minimum. I'll have to order in the parts, and with these strikes . . . Are you all right, Monsieur?'

Marc felt his legs giving way beneath him, two big socks filled with sand. He had to sit down on the camper van step. The mechanic looked at him closely.

'It's not that bad. You know, we fit new engines all the time.'

That was not the problem. His legs were playing the same trick on him as they had done at Laugnac, the same numb sensation that had been swiftly followed by paralysis. Within the hour, he would no longer be able to move. Total breakdown, barely five hundred metres from Agen's exit sign . . . This was looking very much like the end of the road. He would be going no further, he had arrived.

'I'll need to think about it. Can we leave the van here?'

'No, I've got no space. But a little way up on the left there's a disused factory. You could park in the forecourt for the time being. Your van will get you there, but probably not any further.'

'Anne, how long have we been here?'

'About ten days, maybe longer.'

Marc glanced out of the window of the camper van. A two-metre-high wall constructed of breeze blocks and covered in graffiti tags ran towards a patch of no man's land on which the grass was as rusty as the scrap iron strewn over it. When he awoke each morning, Marc's only view was of this wall, this wasteland his only horizon. He and Anne were like castaways, gradually becoming used to the confines within which they now lived. They had made no decisions or plans. They had settled here, like question marks at the end of a sentence.

'We're down to our last twenty euros.'

'That's not much.'

'No, it's not.'

'I'm sorry. We can't use my card any more, of course; it would be too risky. Take my watch, I don't need it.'

'Give it here and I'll see what Tito says. There's some bread and Laughing Cow if you're hungry.'

'See you later.'

*

Tito was their neighbour. He was squatting in a portacabin at the other end of the wasteland. When they first moved in, he had not seemed especially thrilled about it. He kept his distance and went straight past them on his old moped without so much as glancing in their direction. Then one day Anne had asked him if he knew anyone who might want to buy the spare wheel from the van. Tito had sorted it out for them and refused to take a cut. That was how they had got to know one another. He could have been anything from thirty to sixty years old, and his lack of teeth made his accent difficult to place. Besides, he didn't talk much. Every evening he would light a fire and sit for hours gazing at it with a glass of wine. He often shared the food he had salvaged from supermarket bins, asking for nothing in return. He had never tried to find out how they had ended up in this dead end, nor why they seemed in no hurry to leave. He was equally tight-lipped on the subject of his own life. He was someone who had clearly been around the block a few times, and somehow got lost on the way home. His resourcefulness kept them going, and his presence was reassuring. He and Boudu were thick as thieves. Tito always saved a nice titbit for Boudu, who returned the favour by hunting the rats around his portacabin. Each new morning pushed doomsday back another day – not that anyone here seemed too concerned about the world ending.

'About ten days,' Anne had said, 'maybe longer.' She could have told him forty-eight hours or six months, what difference did it make? Yet time had passed. The proof was that his finger had now completely healed over. The tip was still a little sensitive, but he could move it backwards and forwards. Not that this was especially helpful. In the end he had forgotten about it and now only used the finger for minor tasks such as scratching his nose or an ear lobe. The remaining nine fingers more than sufficed for fiddlier jobs, like this embroidery depicting a splendid, almost life-size, horse's head.

Propped up with pillows, Marc spread his sewing kit in front of him. Tito had retrieved the embroidery set from the bin of a haberdashery shop that was closing down. The plastic packaging was still intact and held the painted canvas, a whole assortment of brightly coloured wools, needles and an instruction booklet. Tito had initially offered it to Anne.

'What's this shit for?'

'To make a pretty picture.'

'Look at me, Tito. Do I look like someone who wants to embroider a horse's head?'

Bruised, Tito turned to Marc.

'Want it?'

'But . . . absolutely! It'll keep me busy. Thank you, Tito.'

The horse's head was as ugly as the one Chloé had hung behind the toilet door, of the same conquering breed with flared nostrils, flowing mane and bulging eye, festooned in garish colours. Marc had got started on it that very evening and had continued to work on it increasingly passionately every day since, forcing himself to rein in his enthusiasm so as not to finish it too quickly. He sewed as slowly as a miser counts his gold, point by point, even going as far as to redo some stitches he judged too slack, in order to prolong the pleasure. Alas the project was already three-quarters complete. He would confine himself to the nostrils today, specifically the one on the left.

As the needle came and went through the brown cloth, Marc let his mind wander. The things going through his head were not, strictly speaking, thoughts, but rather random snapshots of apparently unimportant moments in his life, scattered pieces of a puzzle that sometimes came together to form a semblance of coherence. Small things . . . the taste of the langoustines at that dinner party when he had cried out 'I know Agen, too!' . . . Marc held the needle suspended, the thread taut, and burst out laughing. You bet he knew Agen! One day, everyone would know Agen. It was the impression they had of it that was all wrong. Zoltan, the pizza guy, Désiré – none of these people could have guessed what a crucial role Agen would play in their destinies. You casually invoke Agen at a dinner party, never imagining you are actually invoking it, which is quite different.

Marc laid his handiwork on his belly. Boudu was dreaming at the foot of the bed, grinding his teeth and whimpering, his lips, ears and whiskers quivering. It was a moment of almost total peace, before the bubble burst with the screech of tyres. Then came voices, voices which belonged to neither Anne nor Tito. They were prowling around the camper van. Two men. Boudu had pricked up his ears and was turning them round like radars. This was the first time that outsiders had ventured this way. Marc watched as the door handle was lowered and the door opened on a bearded face which, at the sight of Marc, said, 'Jos, there's someone here.'

Another face appeared behind the first, but it was hard to make out with the light behind it.

'On your own in there, Monsieur?'

'Yes. What do you want?'

'Nothing to be afraid of, we're police. We've had your vehicle reported. Have you been here a while?'

'I broke down. Ten or so days ago.'

'There's a garage down the road.'

'I know, but . . . I'm waiting for money to get the engine fixed.'

'Can you stand up, please?'

'No, I'm disabled.'

'Oh. So who's the driver?'

'My daughter. She's gone out.'

'Can I see some ID?'

Marc took his wallet from under his pillow. Struggling to stop his hand from shaking, he gave his identity card to the tall bearded man, who stood beside the bed examining it. After five minutes, he gave it back.

'Everything is in order, Monsieur Lecas. Do you intend to stay here much longer?'

'Just long enough to get the money to have the van fixed. Soon.'

'Soon . . . From what we've been told, you've been parked

here almost three weeks.'

'Is that against the law?'

'Not really. Are you in financial difficulty?'

'What makes you think that?'

'Three weeks on this wasteland. There are better places to go on holiday.'

'It's temporary. A problem with my bank. It'll sort itself out.'

'I hope so. Where were you heading?'

'To Spain.'

'Sightseeing?'

'Yes.'

'Beautiful country, Spain.'

How irritating it was, the way the man punctuated every sentence with a crooked grin and a stroke of his beard. What was keeping him from disappearing back to his world of right and wrong? His sidekick reappeared in the doorway.

'Nothing to report, Antoine.'

The bearded man gave a knowing nod.

'Well, since everything seems to be all right here, we'll leave you be, Monsieur Lecas. We'll stop by again. It's not the safest area, round here. They cleaned things up a bit, got the dealers out, but they could come back anytime. Bye, then. Take care!'

'You need to get out of here, Anne. They're coming back, they said so.'

'No way. I'm happy here. I've got my father, my cat, my friend Tito and a place I like. Why would I fuck off somewhere else?'

'They took down my identity. I'm sure they suspect something. If they come back, they'll arrest us.'

'So what's new? We've already come to the end of the line. Agen, terminus, all change! You say the same thing every single day: we can't go any further, this is it, our "far, far away"; there's nowhere else to go.'

'For me, Anne, only for me! I don't care if I go to prison, but you could make a go of it somewhere else, start again . . .'

'Start again? Start what again? Haven't I done enough of that? I'm sick of your "somewhere elses". That's what got us here, you wanting to take a hike. For the first time in my life, I'm happy where I am, so I'm staying put, and that's final.'

Anne had put on her stubborn face, brow low, nostrils

pinched, lips pouting. For ten minutes she had been battling with a jar of rollmops that refused to open.

'Fuck this!'

She grabbed a hammer in exasperation and, using a knife as a chisel, smashed open the lid in three blows. Marc watched her with a mixture of horror and admiration. She was like a ship's figurehead, impervious to the mightiest of tempests. How had he engendered such a daughter? He tried in vain to think what she had inherited from him. Everything he had never dared to do, perhaps? A wave of tenderness rocked his heart.

'If you're staying because of me . . .'

'You're getting old, my poor Marco. I don't like old age – you get ugly, you hurt all over and you're close to death. Stop talking such crap. No one cares about your two cops. You're sewing your horse's head, Boudu's catching rats, and Tito and I are doing a bit of business. That's life, real life, the only life there is. By the way, your watch wasn't gold.'

The set of slightly too large false teeth, for which Tito had swapped a brand-new kitchen tap, gave him a fixed grin and the pronunciation of a badly tuned radio.

'Before, yes, there were a lot of junkies here. Always fighting, shouting, being sick. Sometimes dying. It was too much. Even I was glad the police cleaned the place up. They're all right, you know, the cops. We're friends. Don't worry, Marc. They come back and I'll talk to them. No problem.'

Tito took out his dentures to try a rollmop. Using his teeth, Marc cut the yarn with which he had finished his horse's nostrils. Anne looked up from the magazine she was flicking through.

'What did I tell you? No problem.'

Tito carefully wiped his fingers on the inside of his jacket and readjusted his teeth, making them chatter several times.

'Anne, what's that thing next to you?'

'An African fetish.'

'Can I see?'

Tito weighed the object in his hand, stretching out his arm and shutting one eye to take a closer look at it.

'I've seen ones like this in the ethnic shop in town. They cost a lot of money. Almost exactly the same, with nails sticking out.'

In Tito's great paws, the statuette looked tiny, curled up on itself like a mummified foetus. It almost seemed afraid. Peering over his glasses, Marc caught Anne's gaze.

'It's meant to bring you good luck, isn't it?'

'Depends who you ask.'

'If you ask me it's an expensive bit of wood.'

'If you sell it, we split it fifty–fifty.'

'We'll see . . .'

Tito put the figure back on top of the fridge.

'I'll take it to the shop tomorrow. Marc, finished the horse's head?'

'Oh yes.'

'Nice work!'

'Keep it. It's for you.'

'Thank you, thank you. I'll put it by my bed. But now you've finished it, what are you going to do?'

The moon was full to bursting. Lying still against one another on the bed, Anne and Marc watched wordlessly as its milky light crept into the camper van. Despite the close quarters, it was like a cathedral, the two of them stretched out like recumbent effigies en route to everlasting life. Marc remembered a painting he had seen in an art magazine. It showed two adolescent boys lying in the bottom of a boat on a calm river. A huge sky stretched above them, marbled pink and grey, and the riverbanks were lined with tall, brooding trees. Curiously enough, this painting, which gave off such an impression of calm and contentment, was entitled *The Unnerved*. Reading the accompanying article, he learned that the scene had been inspired by the legend of a king's two sons who had tried to overthrow him. When the king got wind of their plot, he had them 'unnerved', meaning he had the tendons in their ankles cut so they could no longer walk, before having them thrown into a boat and left at the mercy of the current.

Was this not what he was experiencing with Anne: the thrill of drifting away for ever? Marc propped himself up on his elbow. Anne's face was as serene as those of the boys in the painting, only she was crying. There were no sobs, just an outpouring of tears which looked, in the white light, like drops of mercury rolling along her cheekbone, following the line of her nose, pausing at the corner of her mouth and disappearing in the crook of her neck. Raindrops on a windowpane. She must have felt his gaze on her and turned towards him without trying to hide her pain, but offering it to him as if opening a door.

'Anne . . . is there anything I can do?'

'Yes. Put your arms around me.'

Clumsily, he pulled her towards him. Anne rested her cheek on his chest and wrapped her arm around his waist. He barely dared breathe, his blood rushing to his head.

'Have you ever wondered if I'm really your daughter?'

She said this softly, but her mouth was so close to Marc's heart that her words left him reeling.

'No, never. You *are* my daughter.'

'How can you be so sure? You know Édith as well as I do.'

'I'm not sure where you're going with this.'

'Do you think we look alike? Look at my mouth – it's not your mouth. I don't have your nose either, or eyes, or hair, nothing!'

'You're talking nonsense. Of course you're my daughter. And even if you weren't, I've always thought of you as mine.'

Anne held him more tightly.

'Thought of me . . . but not loved me.'

'Anne! . . . What are you doing?'

'Just relax. I'm going to teach you how to love me. You have to love me. You at least owe me that, don't you?'

'Anne, it's . . . We can't . . . I can't!'

'Of course you can, the proof's right here in my hand. Relax . . .'

'Anne, I'm your father, your real father. Don't . . .'

Anne sat up. Her face was so close to Marc's it blotted out everything else. Her mouth and eyes were wide open, and he stared into a bottomless pit where even darkness had ceased to exist.

'OK! You're my father and I'm your daughter. So what? I have a right to know where I came from, don't I? I want to know if you came when you were making me, because you see I've never been able to, not with anyone. Anyone! Ever! I want to know what it's like, and you're the one who's going to show me. You're the one who wanted me to come with you to places you'd never been. Well here we are. Now it's your turn.'

'You're scaring me, Anne . . .'

'Love me, damn it!'

Marc had the impression his eyes were about to pop out of their sockets like two hard-boiled eggs when Anne grabbed him by the throat. The pressure of her fingers on his Adam's apple made him feel as if he were choking on a ping-pong ball. He felt Anne's other hand thrust his penis inside her. Above his nose, her breasts were bouncing in time. The blood was pounding in his temples, beating an incessant rhythm, tom-tom, jungle sounds, animal grunts, rustling leaves, throbbing sap. Fear had given way to a survival instinct accentuated by pleasure. Waving his hand in the air, it landed on the fetish.

Anne didn't cry out. She bucked one last time and fell onto him. A warm liquid trickled from her lower abdomen. For the first and last time in her life.

Sitting at Marc's bedside, her face puffy with tears, Chloé dabbed at her nose with a tissue.

'How did we get to this point? How could we . . .'

Even if his aching throat had permitted him to speak, Marc would not have known how to reply. Why was she saying 'we'? Who was she talking about – the two of them, or the world in general? And which point had we got to? Agen? A hospital room? The beginning of another conundrum? This apparently simple question was a minefield, riddled with pitfalls from end to end, and Marc didn't feel able to come to his wife's aid.

He had barely recognised her when the police officer had brought her into his room. She looked terribly old. For the past twenty-four hours, the people looking after him – the police, nurses and doctors – had all been incredibly young. Chloé seemed out of place. Why had they brought her all the way here? It was cruel. She must have travelled through the night, found herself a hotel in this unfamiliar town. All alone . . . He had nothing to say to her. Not to her, nor to anyone.

From the moment the inspectors had pulled him, half suffocated, from beneath Anne's body, Marc understood that any attempt at an explanation would be in vain. Besides, his crushed Adam's apple left him barely enough space to breathe. The police officers had had a hell of a time prising Anne's fingers from around his neck. It must be morning, everything was fuzzy, as if seen through a veil. He could make out figures, voices . . .

'Jesus, that was a close call! He's all blue. Monsieur . . .? Can you hear me?'

The camper van was swaying. Marc's head was thrown about on the pillow like a jar of water sloshing from side to side.

'According to Tito, she's his daughter.'

'What a family! He's still got a hard-on, the prick. Monsieur, can you hear me?'

'Look, here come the white coats.'

How could so many people be moving around in so little space? Between his eyelashes, he saw the soles of Anne's feet passing under his nose, sticking out of a survival blanket along with her left hand, which was still gripping an invisible prey. He tried to sit up to get a look at her face, but they held him down and put a rubber face mask on him.

'Don't try to move, Monsieur. Breathe deeply . . . That's it . . .'

Then they put him onto a stretcher. As they made their way out of the van, one of the stretcher-bearers stumbled.

'Shit! What the hell's this?'

Marc saw the fetish roll under the fridge. Outside, with the dark sky behind them, he had met the gazes of Tito and of Boudu, who was nestled in Tito's arms. Both were equally stony-faced, in the way of those who have seen it all before. He smiled at them, but with the mask in the way, they probably didn't see. The two of them were meant for each other, since they had nothing to say to one another. Then everything was white, nothing but white, as if he were drifting along on an ice float.

'Please, Madame, it's time to go.'

'Yes. Yes, of course.'

Chloé's lips felt icy against his forehead. She squeezed his hands.

'I'm here, darling. I'm here . . .'

Marc made a lame attempt at a smile. He was here no longer. When the door closed behind her, he couldn't help breathing a sigh of relief. The nurse leaned in:

'They mean well, but they don't understand.'

She had a very pretty smile, fresh and full of white teeth lined up like chinaware in a shop window.

'Right, then. Could you say something, just one word, without forcing your voice.'

A word? Marc tried to find one in the shiny expanse of the ceiling. Then, having found none, he looked down and his gaze fell on the badge pinned to the nurse's chest.

'Anne.'

C'est la Vie

Pascal Garnier

Translated by Jane Aitken

Writer Jeff Colombier is not accustomed to success. Twice divorced with a grown-up son he barely sees, he drinks too much and his books don't sell.

Then he wins a big literary prize and his life changes for ever. Overwhelmed by his newfound wealth and happiness, he feels the need to escape and recapture his lost youth, taking his son, Damien, with him. And if strange encounters lead them down dangerous paths … well, c'est la vie.

ISBN 9781910477762

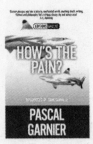

How's the Pain?
Pascal Garnier
Translated by Emily Boyce

Death is Simon's business. And now the ageing vermin exterminator is preparing to die. But he still has one last job down on the coast, and he needs a driver.

Bernard is twenty-one. He can drive and he's never seen the sea. He can't pass up the chance to chauffeur for Simon, whatever his mother may say.

As the unlikely pair set off on their journey, Bernard soon finds that Simon's definition of vermin is broader than he'd expected . . .

New edition with an introduction by John Banville
Published July 2020

ISBN 9781910477922